BUFFALO SOLDIER: ESCORT DUTY

CHARLES RAY

North Potomac, MD

This book is a work of fiction. Names, descriptions, places, and incidents are products of the author's imagination, or are used fictionally. Any resemblance to actual events or persons, living or dead, is purely coincidental.

For information about this and other works of this author, contact the author at charlesray.author@yahoo.com.

Printed in the United States of America.

ISBN: 0615890121
ISBN-13: 978-0615890128 (Uhuru Press)

Buffalo Soldier: Escort Duty

DEDICATION

To the brave soldiers of the United States Colored Troops (USCT), the Ninth and Tenth Cavalry Regiments, and the Twenty-fourth and Twenty-fifth Infantry Regiments, who helped to open the western frontier for the expansion of this country from Atlantic to Pacific. Like those soldiers of color who followed them, they often sacrificed to provide freedom and security for others when they didn't have it themselves.

1.

"You mind tellin' me just how this is a reward?" Sergeant George Toussaint said as he approached Ben Carter. His dark face was twisted in frustration and the beginning of anger. "I ain't had to do work like this since I was a kid and had to tend my grandma's chickens."

It wasn't the first time since sunup that Toussaint had approached Ben to complain. And, Ben knew that the others in the detachment felt the same; they only let Toussaint voice their complaints.

They were only in the third hour of an assignment to escort a work detail that was in a forested area north of Fort Union cutting kindling to be used by the cooks and laundresses. The ten of them and fifteen recruits who were under the supervision of an old sergeant who spent his time napping in the back of one of the two wagons they'd brought along to haul the kindling.

Ben had to admit that it was boring duty, but duty was duty.

"We're just doing this today," he said. "The way they're cutting we should be on the way back to the fort just after noon."

He pointed to the fifteen men who had cut down several medium sized trees, and were in the process of chopping them into smaller chunks. The cut wood was stacked in piles which would then be put on the two wagons.

"I don't see why we have to watch over them," Toussaint said. "Why can't they take care of themselves? They's cavalrymen just like us."

"It's not for us to be questioning orders."

And, the order had come from the Troop commander, Major Joshua Wainwright, the day before. He'd approached Ben in the stable as he was brushing his horse.

"Sergeant Carter," Wainwright said. "I was hoping I'd catch you here."

Ben stopped what he was doing and stood to attention.

"Yes sir, major," he said. "What can I do for you?"

"Actually, sergeant, it's what I can do for you."

"Do for me, sir? I don't understand. I don't really need anything."

Wainwright laughed and clapped Ben on the shoulder.

"The colonel and I were discussing you, and that's what he said you'd say. But, son, you do need something."

"What's that, sir?"

"You and that detachment of yours have been deployed to the field almost continuously since we moved here. You men have seen more action than almost anyone else in the regiment, and the colonel feels you need a break. And, frankly I agree."

"Most of the men just had leave, sir," Ben said. "And, I don't really need any time off right now."

"Oh, we weren't thinking about giving you vacation time, sergeant. No, the colonel had lighter duty in mind for you. Get you out of the field for a few weeks."

The image of garrison duty flashed through Ben's mind. It wasn't exactly what he considered *light* duty, and he doubted if the men of the detachment would be too happy being stuck at the fort running errands for officers or doing household chores.

"I appreciate that, sir," he said. "But, we like being in the field. I don't think we'd be too good at garrison duty."

"We weren't exactly thinking of normal garrison duty, sergeant," Wainwright said. "You might call it modified field duty. It was the colonel's idea, really, but I totally agree."

"I'm afraid you got me confused, major. How can it be light duty out of the field, but not be garrison duty?"

"Of course, you've been in the field so much, you wouldn't know what's been happening around here. Some of our work details have been harassed by locals, mostly drunk cowboys, and our supply wagons have been attacked by robbers on occasion. The colonel had the idea of having armed escorts with them to prevent that, and with the combat experience you and your men have had, you're the perfect unit to do it."

"You want us to do escort duty?"

"That's right, Sergeant Carter. As of tomorrow, your detachment is the official escort for work details and supply convoys leaving Fort Union. You can report to the adjutant for the particulars."

Wainwright then spun on his heels and walked away, leaving Ben standing in the stable with his mouth open. When the officer was out of sight, Ben shook himself. He thought about this new job he'd been assigned. It was unusual, but it made a kind of sense. And, maybe it wouldn't be too bad. They wouldn't have to be getting shot at all the time; and they wouldn't be stuck in the fort doing menial labor. He was sure the men would like it.

In that he was completely wrong. Just hours into their first escort mission, and the men hated it.

"So, what they gone have us doin' next?" Toussaint asked.

"I'm not sure," Ben replied. "The adjutant said we might have to escort the mail wagon to Santa Fe tomorrow, but I'll have to check with him when we get back to the fort to be sure."

"Well now, that wouldn't be too bad. I wouldn't mind goin' up to Santa Fe."

"Wouldn't be much time to do more than drop off the mail, pick up whatever they got for the fort and head back."

"Surely there'd be time for a good steak dinner? You wouldn't begrudge a man a good steak dinner, would you?"

Ben laughed. "No, I reckon I could allow time for that," he said.

Heck, he thought, wouldn't mind a nice juicy steak myself. The cooks at Fort Union ain't bad, but they can't cook steak worth a nickel.

Placated at the thought of a trip to the territorial capital, Toussaint rode off to share the news with the others. Ben found himself hoping the adjutant wouldn't change his mind and send them on another wood cutting detail. He'd never hear the last of it.

Ben urged his horse forward, in the direction of three recruits who were chipping branches into manageable sized kindling. As he approached, the men stopped working and looked up at him, broad smiles on their dark faces.

"Hey, sergeant," one man said. "You want to git a little exercise? We sho could use some hep with this here kindlin'."

"No," Ben replied. "I have to keep watch so no outlaws or Indians sneak up on you while you're workin'. 'Sides, looks like you're about done."

"Yeah, we'se gone be stoppin' for vittles soon, and it won't be soon enough for me. I'se so hungry, my stomach's gnawin' at my rib cage."

"I'm hungry too," another soldier said. "And, I got me a feelin' for some music after eatin'."

"Then, you in luck," the first soldier said. "I

done brought my mouth organ wit me today. We kin have a little shindig after we eats."

"Sho nuff? Now, that sound like a mighty fine idea," the third soldier said. I saw a holler log what would make a good drum. I kin play 'long wit you."

"Then, we gone have us a shindig and a fine meal. Now, that be livin'."

Ben winced as they spoke. While it wasn't uncommon for the troopers of the cavalry to stage impromptu entertainment, often for the amusement for their white officers, but mostly for their own diversion, the men of his detachment, especially George Toussaint, cringed every time it happened. Toussaint was reminded of his time on the riverboats, when he'd often be forced to buck dance for the white patrons who would throw pennies at him, and whenever the men in the fort would start playing, he would go off by himself to avoid seeing it. Ben feared that if the work detail started singing and dancing, even though there were no whites around to see, it would set Toussaint off. The big sergeant had been known to grab harmonicas or fiddles from troopers and smash them, precipitating free-for-alls that had to be broken up sometimes by nearly breaking a few heads. An incident on their first assignment was the last thing Ben wanted or needed. If this current assignment was to be successfully concluded, he would have to go the extra mile to avoid any kind of confrontation. That meant ensuring that Toussaint was nowhere near the mess area.

He rode away from the three soldiers who were now talking excitedly about their planned entertainment, in the direction he'd seen Toussaint go. He would suggest that he and the sergeant stand sentry duty out to the east of the work area, the direction that trouble was most likely to come from, eating in the saddle.

Dang if it's not easier to command men when you're getting shot at, Ben thought as he rode. *This easy duty's about as easy as pushing a rope up a hill.*

2.

The best plan in the world falls apart if you fail to consider every factor that has an impact on it. Ben had failed to take into account that sound, especially drumbeats, the wail of a harmonica, and several voices raised in song, traveled a long way, and he'd not taken Toussaint far enough away from the camp site to be out of range of the music and singing. It came through clearly to where they sat with their backs against a boulder, eating the dried beef and hard biscuits that constituted their mid-day meal.

When the first notes of music drifted in on the air, Ben tensed and watched his friend out of the corner of his eye. Toussaint's eyes narrowed, and a muscle in his dark cheek started twitching, but he said nothing.

"I gone lay down my burden, down by the rivuh side, down by the rivuh side, way down by the rivuh side."

The words came clearly, with one particularly deep bass voice prominent over the mournful sound of the harmonica. As Ben watched Toussaint, in addition to the anger, he saw sadness in the man's eyes. He could understand that. Both he and Toussaint had been mere children when the Civil War ended, ending the peculiar institution of slavery, but he still remembered.

He remembered the stories, whispered to him late at night by his father and mother, about the slaves and their desire to escape to freedom, and their resentment at being treated on a par with the livestock, or in some cases even less. Songs were used to signal escape plans or routes for those who wanted to take their freedom into their own hands. Often their desire would be reflected in the songs they sang, using cryptic words and phrases to avoid punishment by their masters.

Unlike slaves in other southern states, who sought freedom in the northern states and Canada, most slaves in Texas sought the friendly environment of Mexico to the south, where the government honored their rights as human beings and welcomed them. Some sought refuge with the East Texas Indian tribes where, even though they weren't treated as equals, they attained a degree of freedom and dignity. Those who went south, went through the Coastal Bend, braving lakes infested with alligators, and into the Nueces Desert, where they endured intense heat, poisonous snakes, and lack of water. Throughout their journey they had to dodge gangs of slave hunters and along the Rio Grande, bands of cannibalistic Karankawa Indians.

As a child, Ben could never understand how people who endured the indignity and suffering of slavery could sing and dance, but as he grew older, he realized that this was their way of coping, and easing their burdens.

George Toussaint, he reckoned, had not come to that realization. He still seemed to hold a deep resentment of anything that reminded him of the dark period of slavery.

Ben let him stew in silence. He noticed that when the kindling and tools were loaded on the wagons and the work party headed back to the fort, Toussaint rode far out ahead, avoiding eye contact with everyone.

He and his detachment separated from the work party when they arrived at Fort Union, leaving the recruits to take the kindling to the wood storage area, while they went directly to the stables to take care of their horses and gear.

After taking care of his horse, Ben reported to the adjutant who confirmed that their duty the next day would be to escort the mail wagon to Santa Fe and back. He breathed a sigh of relief.

The evening meal was quiet, or as quiet as a crowd of hungry soldiers can ever be. Ben and his men sat apart from the others; they'd taken to doing that after their second mission. The other troopers recognized them as special, and didn't seem to mind, and truth be told, most of them were skittish around Toussaint and Corporals Lucas Hall and Charles Buckley anyway.

When they finished eating, they all went back to the barracks for single soldiers, which they shared with ten other troopers who mostly ignored them, but who were out in the quadrangle formed by the barracks, quarters for married troopers and laundry sheds singing, talking, and playing cards. Excited at the prospect of going to Santa Fe, Ben and his men were preparing their gear, shining leather and polishing metal to a high sheen.

"Can't have troopers from the Ninth ridin' into Santa Fe lookin' sloppy," Corporal Journeyman Keller said as he slapped beeswax on his boots and began rubbing it in.

"We'd better get to sleep early tonight," Ben said. "Mail wagon driver likes to head out right after breakfast, so we need to get our horses and gear ready before we eat in the mornin'."

The sun hadn't yet risen when Ben got up the next morning and quietly roused his detachment. Most of the men were already awake. They were excited about going to Santa Fe. After getting their horses, weapons, and gear settled, they ate a quick breakfast, mounted and rode toward the main gate where they were to meet the mail wagon.

At the gate, they found not one, but two, wagons. Each had two passengers, a driver and an armed trooper riding shotgun, and was pulled by a team of four horses. The first wagon was driven by a Mexican who introduced himself as Cesar Ortega, one of the fort's civilian drovers. The shotgun was a lanky, dark skinned corporal named Peter Collier. The cargo consisted of several canvas bags securely fastened. This, Ben knew was the outgoing mail, personal letters and official dispatches. The second wagon, with two armed troopers, Private Moses Lake and Corporal Robert Alexander, was empty.

"Why the extra wagon?" Ben asked Collier as he rode up at the head of the detachment.

"Cap'n say we might have a extra heavy load to bring back," the corporal answered. "Ain't that right, Cesar?"

"Si," the Mexican drover answered. "El Capitan, he say, one wagon not enough."

Ben shrugged. It would mean stretching out

the detachment over a wider distance to cover both wagons. Some of the territory they had to traverse consisted of narrow canyons, which would make this a risky formation. But, if the officer in charge had ordered it, there was little he could do but make the best of it.

"Okay," he said. "Keep about twenty yards between wagons so the ones behind don't have to eat too much dust." He turned to his detachment. "Samuel, you and Malachi ride point. George, you ride just in front of the lead wagon. Nat and Marcus, ride trail, about twenty, thirty yards back. Rest of you, split up and ride flank. I'll be moving back and forth to keep an eye on things."

"Is that really necessary, sergeant?" Collier asked. "I mean, I been doin' the mail run for two month now, and ain't never had no trouble."

"If we're ready, won't be trouble this time either," Ben said. "All right, everyone take your positions."

Hightower and Davis rode up and stationed themselves about twenty yards in front of the lead wagon. Toussaint eased his horse just in front of and off to the side. Tatum and Scott fell in behind the second wagon. The rest moved to the flanks, two to the left and three to the right. Ben decided he would ride to the left to balance the flank on that side.

"Okay, let's move out," he said.

With the wagons creaking and rumbling, the convoy moved past the main gate of Fort Union and headed southwest toward the capital. With the wagons, especially the one loaded down with mail bags, Ben knew they'd be lucky to make 45 miles per day, taking them two days to travel the 95 miles from Fort Union to Santa Fe. His plan was to follow the trail south through the town of Las Vegas, and stop for a night camp about 20 miles southeast of town. Starting the next morning at dawn, they could make Santa Fe before dark, while the railroad depot was still open.

They passed through Las Vegas just after three in the afternoon. Founded in 1835 by settlers who'd received a land grant from Mexico, it was one of the largest towns in the territory. It was laid out in traditional Spanish colonial style, with a broad central plaza surrounded by buildings that served as fortifications in the event of Indian attack. They rode past the place where General Stephen Watts Kearny had claimed New Mexico for the United States in 1846, a part of the plaza where locals had set up small flower and vegetable markets.

One of the main stops on the Santa Fe Trail, Las Vegas had attracted businessmen as well as outlaws. As they passed the site of construction of the new railway station, Ben mused on the fact that when completed it would mean a shorter ride to pick up the fort's mail, but would also expose the cavalry troopers to more robbers, murderers, and con men, the dregs of society that inevitably followed the railroad as surely as the robber barons and business men who became rich from the iron road that was slowly knitting the country together from east to west. Already, Ben and his men observed as their convoy passed through the town, there were a few Victorian-style mansions indicating the presence of someone of wealth. The opulence of the mansions contrasted sharply with the adobe dwellings of the majority of the town's less prosperous residents.

The streets were crowded with people, most of whom paid little attention to the wagons and their cavalry escort, which suited Ben well. He'd never become accustomed to the hostility some of the territory's settlers had toward the black men of the Ninth, even though the cavalry was there to protect them.

By the time they arrived at Bernal Springs, where the trail cut west and northwest, the sun was low in the sky and casting long shadows, and the mountain range was purple in the distance.

Ben raised his hand for a halt, and called the point riders back.

"Okay, we'll stop here for the night," he said.

"If we start out as sunup tomorrow, we ought to be in Santa Fe by mid-afternoon."

"Fine by me," Toussaint said, as he rode up to Ben. "My backside could use a rest."

Ben laughed. He knew all the men were probably a bit saddle sore. It had been a while since they'd had to spend so much time in the saddle. As the men rode up and dismounted, and the wagon drivers jumped down from the seats, he explained how he wanted the camp laid out.

He had the two wagons placed back-in, perpendicular to each other, forming two sides of a square, or a 'V' shape. The horses were tethered at the open end, and he assigned the Mexican drover the duty of watching out for them. A few feet beyond the tethered beasts he directed a camp fire be built, and directed the men to arrange their sleeping rolls in a staggered row between the fire and wagons.

Two of the troopers who'd been riding the wagons grumbled at having to undergo such ritual just for a one-night camp.

"Do it anyway," Ben said. "This way, when we're on the way back, you can do it without having to think about it. Set up like this, if we're attacked, we can quickly move and use the wagons for cover on one side and the horses on the other."

"And, if you don't do it," Toussaint said with a growl. "I just might make you wish the Apaches attacked us."

With wide eyes, the two men rushed to comply with Ben's instructions.

"Not exactly the way I would have handled it," Ben said wryly.

"I know," Toussaint said. "But, I figured you didn't want to have to spend half the night convincin' 'em to do the right thing."

3.

After a quick breakfast in the dark, Ben had the camp fire doused and got the convoy back on the road. The path wound upwards, with the southern end of the Sangre de Cristo Mountains on their right and the flat tops of Glorieta Mesa on their left.

The orange sun from their rear cast long shadows on the trail ahead. They passed through Pecos Canyon just before topping the final rise leading into the territorial capital. Smaller than Las Vegas, Santa Fe had been the capital of the area since it was under Spanish control. Beds of cactus lined the road in places, knee-high round green leafed plants with long, sharp spines, and in others waist-high grass undulated in the breeze. Now and then wagon tracks or a single trail broke off the main trail leading to homesteads hidden in distant groves of hardwood trees. As they got closer to the outskirts of town, they saw houses nearer the trail. Some were the fine *haciendas* of wealthy ranchers. Others were humble adobe huts belonging to those who worked the land for others.

They came into town from the south, passing the San Miguel Mission at the south side of town, and the Governor's Palace, which had served as the town's administrative center since Spanish days, before coming to the rail depot. The depot was small for a territorial capital, but the mountainous terrain around the city had caused the railroad to decide to serve it via a trunk line rather than try and cut the main line through the precipitous terrain.

A rat-faced clerk, who seemed put out at having to stay a few minutes late to receive the army mail, took possession of the Fort Union mail bags, locking them in a large room in the back of the depot, and giving Ben a receipt.

After putting the horses and wagons up at a livery stable near the depot, they walked to a nearby hotel and were lucky enough to be able to get rooms for the entire group. After settling their gear, they split up to enjoy an evening on the town. Ben and George Toussaint walked along the dusty sidewalk to a saloon near the hotel.

The place wasn't crowded. Most of the patrons looked to be cowboys from ranches in the area with a few townspeople sprinkled in among them. A skinny man wearing a top hat and black coat with tails, sat at a piano in the corner playing one discordant song after another, which the patrons ignored.

"You want a table or is the bar okay?" Toussaint asked.

There were only a few cowboys at the bar, standing at one end drinking. The empty tables, though, were all near someone, and Ben preferred solitude.

"End of the bar looks empty," he said. "Let's go there."

The bored looking bartended, a pale, short man with a paunch under his apron like a small melon, took their order of pork chops, biscuits and beer. He brought the beers right away. Ben took a sip.

"Danged if they don't let anybody come in here," a voice behind him said.

Ben turned to see one of the cowboys from the other end of the bar, a tall, gangly man with a pockmarked face and a wispy mustache, standing near him with a scowl on his sun-browned face. He sensed Toussaint's body tensing next to him.

"I'm sorry," Ben said. "Were you talkin' to me?"

The man laughed. A trail of brown spittle snaked from the side of his mouth.

"Naw, boy, I'se talkin' 'bout you." He turned to the bartender. "Charlie, you jest let anything wander in off the street, don't you. Next you be servin' dogs 'n Injuns."

"Now, come on, Billy Ray," the bartender said. "Let's not start no trouble."

"Aw, Charlie, you know me," the cowboy said. "I don't cause no trouble. I jest wants to know how come a white man can't have a peaceful drink with his friends without all the riff-raff comin' in."

"These soldiers ain't botherin' you and your friends, Billy Ray."

"Them jest bein' here bothers me." He turned back to Ben. "Now, boy, why don't you and your friend jest haul your black carcasses on outa here?"

Toussaint stood away from the bar, loosening the flap of his holster. Ben laid a hand on his arm, shaking his head.

"We'll leave as soon as we've eaten our meal," he said to the cowboy.

"I think you gone be leavin' right now, boy." The cowboy turned to his three companions. "What say, boys? We gone show these two darkies the door?"

The three men, almost too drunk to walk straight, shoved away from the bar and started staggering toward their friend.

"I think maybe you boys oughta find somethin' else to amuse you," a deep voice said.

The three men stopped still. The man who'd been taunting Ben and Toussaint paled and his eyes went wide.

Ben hadn't noticed the man in black when he entered the saloon. He'd been sitting alone in a corner table in shadow. Now, he stood next to Ben and Toussaint.

He was tall, well over six feet, with broad shoulders and a narrow waist. He had a narrow face with high cheekbones of leathery, sun-bronzed skin. His eyes were ice blue under dark brown brows that feathered out at the side. A sharp nose swooped straight down to a thin mustache over thin lips which regarded the four drunken cowboys without humor. He was dressed entirely in black; a black hat set squarely on his head, black shirt and black pants. His holster was black leather, and was worn low and strapped to his leg. The butt of his revolver was also black.

"We jest tryin' to keep this a place where decent white men can come to drink," the cowboy said. "It ain't no place for colored folk; 'specially these blue belly soldiers."

"If you wanted to keep it decent," the man in black said; his voice as icy as his blue eyes. "You and your friends would leave. You roughnecks from Texas come here to Santa Fe and bring your filthy habits with you. The only color that counts here is the color of a man's money, and we measure a man by whether or not he's decent. By that standard, you four don't measure up."

"Y-you sidin' with them?"

"What do you think?"

The cowboy, only slightly less drunk than his friends, eyed the gun on the man's hip, and the cold look in his eyes. His friends stood behind him a good distance, waiting to see what he would say. They were just drunk enough, Ben thought, to do something foolish like make a move on the stranger. The way the man wore his gun, the way he stood, the way he talked, all this told Ben that he was no stranger to gunfights, and that if the cowboys did something stupid like attempt to draw on him, it would probably be the last mistake they ever made.

Ben watched as the bravado brought on by too much whisky drained out of the man. He turned to his friends.

"Come on, fellas," he said. "This here pig pen ain't no place for a decent white man. Let's find ourselves another place to drink."

The drunken men gave the man in black a wide berth as they slunk out of the saloon.

Ben turned to the man.

"Thank you, mister," he said. "Mighty kind of you to side with us like that."

The man touched a finger to the brim of his hat.

"No thanks necessary, sergeant," he said. "My name's Palladin, Joshua Palladin; and you might say I was just payin' off a debt I owe."

"I'm Ben Carter, and this is my friend Sergeant George Toussaint," Ben said. "And, I don't know of any debt you owe either of us."

"Oh, not you specific, but I owe you Buffalo Soldiers my life."

"We're cavalrymen," Toussaint said. "Not buffalo hunters."

"Not hunters, soldiers, Buffalo Soldiers" Palladin said. "Didn't you know that's what the Indians out here call you man 'cause of your wooly hair, and they pure dee respect your fightin' ability."

"I didn't know that," Ben said, but his chest swelled with pride at the thought. "How'd the cavalry save your life?"

Palladin walked up to the bar and ordered whisky. After the bartender had poured three fingers of the amber liquor into a glass, he knocked back half before telling his story.

"I'm a bounty hunter by trade," he said. "Work mostly 'round the territory and up north, goin' after horse thieves and bank robbers." He took another sip of whisky. "I was trailin' this gang of stage coach robbers what had been hittin' coaches on the Santa Fe Trail regular like. I thought there was just three of 'em, and that I had 'em cornered up in the Sangre de Cristo Mountains. Only, it turned out there were six, and while I was chasin' three, the other three circled 'round behind me."

"You got ambushed?" Toussaint asked.

"That I did, as sweet as you please. They had me pinned down and caught in a cross fire. Only reason they didn't kill me outright is they were lousy shots, and they started shootin' too early. Gave me a chance to hunker down behind some boulders with a rocky wall to my back. I was runnin' low on ammunition though, and they'd of kilt me for sure if these four cavalry troopers who'd been out lookin' for renegade Indians hadn't come 'long when they did. They attacked the three who'd come at me from behind, and the other three lost stomach for the fight and lit out. I'm standin' here today because of black troopers from the Ninth Cavalry; same outfit as you. Far as I'm concerned, that debt ain't even half paid, and if I can ever do anything for you fellas, you can be sure I will."

Ben thanked Palladin for coming to their aid, and offered to buy him another drink.

"Sergeant, your money's no good in this saloon long's I'm around. Charlie, put their food and drink on my tab."

He touched his right index finger to the brim of his hat again, turned and walked away.

The bartender was putting their food on the bar as the saloon doors swung closed behind Palladin's broad shoulders.

"Dang," Toussaint said, just before diving into his food. "I guess all white folk ain't all that bad."

4.

The encounter with the drunken cowboys and the bounty hunter Palladin was all but forgotten by the following morning. He roused his crew just before sunup, talked the hotel cook into cooking breakfast early for them, retrieved horses and wagons from the livery stable, and was at the railroad depot when the doors opened.

As the men were loading mailbags onto the wagons under the watchful eye of the rat-faced clerk from the previous day, a balding, paunchy clerk with florid cheeks and watery blue eyes summoned Ben into a tiny office in the back of the mail storage room. When Ben entered the man closed the door.

"I got some special cargo, sergeant," the man said. "I can only tell you as the person in charge, and you might want to keep what I tell you to yourself until you get back to Fort Union."

Ben regarded the man with a suspicious glance.

"Special cargo? What kind of special cargo? They didn't say anything about that back at the fort."

"That's 'cause they probably didn't know. It just came in the day before you arrived. I sent a telegram to the fort and they wired back for me to give it to you to deliver. The cargo is cash; two bags of it; for your payroll and such."

Ben had an empty feeling in the pit of his stomach at this news as the man hauled two canvas bags slightly larger than saddle bags from the safe behind the desk that took up most of the space in the room. He put the bags on the desk and picked up a sheet of paper.

"I'm gonna need your signature showin' you received it," he said.

When Ben saw the amount he was signing for, seventy-five thousand dollars, the empty feeling turned to hot lava. He felt as if his breakfast might come back up. It was one thing to be escorting mail, but if word got out somehow that the detachment was escorting this much money every outlaw within a hundred miles would be dogging them. When his hand stopped shaking, he took the pen the man offered and scrawled his signature at the bottom of the document.

The man picked up the bags and handed them to him.

"It's all yours now, sergeant, good luck."

He didn't sound as if he really meant it though.

Ben went back outside where the loading of the regular mail was completed. He pulled Toussaint aside.

"George," he said. "We got these two special bags to carry back to the fort. I'll carry one, and I want you to carry the other, and whatever you do, don't let it get out of your sight."

"What's in it?" Toussaint asked as he took the bag and hefted it over his shoulder. "Too light to be gold."

"Important papers for the regiment," Ben said, regretting having to deceive his friend. "They have to get to the adjutant."

Toussaint nodded and went back to supervising getting the men and wagons lined up for departure. Ben vowed he'd make up for the deception somehow when they got back to Fort Union.

The men were ready to leave, but as Ben was

about to mount, a slightly built man wearing a threadbare gray coat and a battered gray Stetson walked up to him.

"Excuse me, s-sergeant," the man said. "C-could I speak with you a moment?"

"Yes sir, what can I do for you?"

"Well, I heared you was takin' a mail wagon back to Fort Union. My name's Danford, Robert Danford, and I got a little spread over near Las Vegas. I raise horses. I been up here in Santa Fe sellin' some of my stock, and I'm on my way back home with the money and some presents for my little girls. I got two girls, age six and ten, and this'll be the first time I been able to buy 'em somethin' nice, see. Anyway, I was kinda hopin' I could ride 'long with you soldiers as far as my place. Been some robberies 'long that stretch of road, and I don't feel comfortable ridin' it alone."

Ben's first reaction was to say no. He'd have enough just keeping the mail and payroll safe. But, protecting the settlers was one of the cavalry's missions, and if he let the man ride alone and something bad happened, he'd never forgive himself.

"It's a two day ride to Las Vegas," Ben said. He noticed that the man, unlike most men in the region, didn't wear a sidearm. "If you ride with us, you'll have to pull your own weight. Do you have a weapon?"

"I got a Winchester rifle, and I'm a pretty fair shot."

"Okay, you can tag along. Pull your wagon in behind the second one, and when we move out, you listen to what I tell you and do it right away." The man nodded, smiling weakly. "You have to bring your own grub, too. I only got enough for my men."

"That won't be a problem," the man said. The relief in his voice was plain. "I got 'nough, I can share with you fellas."

When Danford's wagon was in place, Ben had the detachment line up, half in front of the lead wagon under his control, the rest behind the last wagon under Toussaint. He patted the bag of money which he'd attached to his saddle, and gave the order to move out.

The group, the three wagons making loud creaking noises, moved through town to the south with everyone in close formation. Ben kept it this way until he could no longer see the spire of the cathedral when he looked over his shoulder. He signaled a stop. He then sent Hightower and Holman forward with instructions to scout the trail ahead about half a mile for any signs of ambush. He sent Tatum and Hall to the rear to do the same. He then had the wagons move so there was about thirty feet between each, placing the rest of the detachment to either side of the first and last wagon and gave the signal to move out.

He then rode to the center of the group and over the noise of the wagons, described how he wanted the wagons handled if he called an alert. He could have stopped the formation to do it more easily, but didn't want to spend any more time on the trail than necessary. At any event, he was able to make himself heard.

His instructions were simple; if he called for an emergency stop, the first wagon would stop where it was; the second would pull to its right and pull alongside, about a wagon's length away. Danford, in the third wagon, would swing around and pull his wagon across behind the other two, forming a three-sided enclosure. The drivers would set the wagon brakes and immediately unhitch the teams, placing them in the open end of the enclosure, securing the animals to the wagon tongues. In the meantime, the cavalrymen would be making firing positions by placing saddle bags and other gear on the ground inside the enclosure.

When he was satisfied that everyone understood his instructions, Ben yelled, "Emergency stop!"

There was momentary confusion as the second wagon started to go left before the driver realized his mistake and pulled the reins hard right. Danford was a bit slow getting his wagon pulled in behind the other two, but with a little pushing and shoving, within five minutes, they had a relatively good little redoubt established. Ben was proud of how well they'd done, having only just heard his instructions, but he scowled at them.

"If we were under attack, some of us would be dead," he said. "We have to do it a lot faster than that. Get the horses hitched back up. Next time, I expect us to be set up in no more than a minute."

The men on the cavalry wagons grumbled, and Danford looked confused. As they set out again, he looked over at Ben. The look on his face made it clear that he was having second thoughts about the wisdom of traveling with the army, at least with that part of it being led by this crazy sergeant.

His feeling was confirmed half an hour later when Ben called another emergency stop, but as Ben had expected, having done it once, it was easier the second time. It only took a bit over a minute. He was satisfied they could do it, but when they set out again, he said nothing. Nor did he answer a question from one of the cavalry drivers who wanted to know how many more times they would have to do his 'stupid' exercise.

Ben had no intentions of doing it again for practice, and hoped circumstances wouldn't make it necessary to do it for real. To keep them ready, though, he said nothing. Best they think he was a bit touched in the head, or crazy with the power of being in command, he thought. If they focused on being mad at him, should they be attacked, they might not panic. The men of his detachment, he knew, would acquit themselves well in a fight, but he was unfamiliar with the other soldiers, and Danford was a civilian who looked as if he'd never seen a shot fired in anger.

Worry gnawed at Ben's gut.

It was like the time when the regiment had still been stationed in Texas, and he'd been sent out to take command of the detachment that had been assigned the task of stopping a band of Comanche warriors who had been terrorizing ranches in the area, or recently when he'd been assigned to lead a group of raw recruits in pursuit of some Apache who had fled the reservation, only worse. In the first case, his worry was that he wouldn't be able to get the men to accept his authority. But, they were at least battle-hardened and experienced. In the second, he worried that the recruits, with their lack of experience, wouldn't be able to handle themselves. But, they at least had the benefit of some military training.

The current situation was far worse in his mind. He now had the responsibility for a civilian with no military training. He couldn't be sure the man would know what to do if they came under attack, and that worried him, because, in addition to fighting off the attack, he would have to keep an eye on him.

He was so worried, when they stopped for the mid-day meal, he only picked at his food, and the coffee he drank only increased the uncomfortable feeling in his stomach.

His problem was compounded by having to conceal his doubts from everyone. It wouldn't do to demoralize the men by having them see that he was beset with self-doubt. He kept his expression stony, his commands crisp, and his shoulders square as they set out after finishing the meal.

5.

As the convoy approached Pecos Canyon, Ben's worry was replaced by a feeling of unease. He couldn't quite pinpoint the source of the unease, but it was definite and strong; an itchy feeling at the nape of his neck, as if thousands of gnats were buzzing around him.

As he scanned the surrounding terrain, he saw nothing to account for the sensation. The sky was bright blue with wispy trails of clouds. The air was warm; a hint of a breeze rolled in from the east keeping it from becoming stifling hot. The jagged walls of the canyon rose on his left, red clay and gray rock mixed in garish combinations, with the occasional splash of green where either cactus or scrub pushed its way up through to the surface. The ground fell off gently to the right, reddish brown earth covered in cactus and scrub. Off in the distance, Ben could see a lone coyote loping along, its nose close to the ground. A hawk made lazy circles above the convoy.

Everything Ben could see and hear made it look like the most peaceful of days; a day when he should enjoy being on the trail; but, he could feel menace in the air, the smell of trouble in his nostrils. It was like the feeling he'd had in the past just before going into combat; but then, he'd known who and where the enemy was. Now, though, he only had the uneasy feeling.

So strong had been that feeling, when they set out after eating, he'd instructed the outriders front and rear to station themselves where they could see the convoy and be seen. He didn't explain why he did this, and his men, accustomed to following his instructions without question, and trusting his instincts, asked for none.

Just as Ben was thinking he might be a touch paranoid, he looked back over his shoulder.

Tatum and Hall, riding abreast, were heading toward them, and they had their horses running flat out. So much for paranoia, Ben thought.

"Convoy, halt," he yelled.

The two corporals pulled their horses up as they neared Ben.

"What's the matter?" Ben asked.

Tatum was the first to catch his breath.

"Riders comin' up behind us," he said. "Was eight at first, but when we started up this last slope, three of 'em must of split off, 'cause I only saw five just now, and they's ridin' this way hard."

That, Ben knew, meant no good.

"Pull the wagons into the emergency stop formation," he ordered.

The drivers, Danford included, immediately began the drill Ben had had them rehearse. The wagons were positioned, brakes locked, and horses tethered to the tongues of the two lead wagons in slightly over a minute. The troopers dismounted, securing their own horses and removed their pack rolls to create barricades and firing platforms.

Hightower and Holman had been looking back from time to time to make sure they stayed in sight of the convoy, and when they saw the wagons begin to move into the defensive formation, wheeled their horses around and rushed back to join the rest.

Everyone was lying on the ground, weapons ready, when the first rider appeared over a little rise in the trail. At first, they only saw his head, but soon rider and horse were silhouetted against the sky, and he was quickly joined by four others. They stopped, just out of carbine range.

"What d-do you t-think they'll do?" Danford asked. He was prone on the dirt next to Ben.

"They'll probably wait until their friends can get around behind us," he said. He wasn't sure, but in their place, it's what he would have done. "Keep a sharp eye out behind us, and let me know if you see anything." That last he directed at George Toussaint, who was guarding the trail to their front with three troopers lying beside him. "Don't shoot, though, until I give the order."

"Got you," was all Toussaint said.

Ben patted the bag of currency he'd put on the ground beside him. Looking back he noticed that Toussaint had put the other bag beside him along with his ammunition pouches.

The five riders sat motionless, appearing to be deep in conversation. Then, they wheeled their horses around and disappeared over the rise.

"Get ready," Ben said. "I think they might be about to make a move."

Just like that, the peaceful scene had been transformed to a battle in the making. Fifteen men, tense and alert, lay on the ground in the makeshift fortress made from the three wagons, their weapons at the ready. The horses, as if sensing the impending peril, whinnied nervously and pawed at the ground.

Ben was no longer worried. As always, just before going into battle, his mind became calm, his breathing steady.

As he watched the point from which the men had disappeared, he noticed a glint, probably the sun flashing off a rifle barrel. They were on the move. He took a deep breath and eased his Springfield over the large pack behind which he lay, looking down the barrel as he aimed it at the rise.

The sound of the bullet smacking into the side of the wagon above him came a second before he heard the sharp crack. He looked quickly from side to side and was rewarded with the sight of a wisp of smoke indicating the shooter's position.

"Hold your fire," he said quietly.

He could sense tension in Danford and the troopers from the wagons. This was probably new to them. His men, though, had been in similar or worse situations many times. He knew he could count on them.

"What do you see back there, George?" he asked.

"Thought I saw a movement 'bout two, three hundred yards back," Toussaint answered.

A geyser of dirt erupted in the cactus field simultaneously with the crack of the shot. The men trying to circle around to cut them off were closer, and therefore more dangerous.

"Shoot back if you have a target," Ben said.

Toussaint made a grunting sound as if to say he already knew to do that.

Ben meanwhile was scanning the ground to his front, looking for any sign of movement, any kind of target, while at the same time watching the civilian who lay next to him, his face ashen with fear.

There was a long moment of silence, which was broken by a ragged volley of fire from the vicinity of the five concealed gunmen. Some of the rounds hit the wagons making a dull thudding sound, while some knocked up dirt and rock around them.

Out of the corner of his eye Ben saw one of the soldiers, the one who'd been on the wagon with the Mexican driver, raise up, his shoulders above the line of packs, aiming his weapon.

"Get down -" Ben started to yell, but there was a sharp crack and the man grabbed his shoulder, rolling over against the soldier beside him.

"Ow, I been hit," the man moaned, clutching at the widening dark spot on his shoulder.

"All of you stay down," Ben said with as much force as he could muster.

He scooted over and look at the man's bleeding shoulder. He could from the hole in the back of his tunic, where blood was already spreading, that the bullet had gone completely through.

"Keep down and see if you can stop the bleeding," he said to the wide-eyed Mexican. He put a hand on the wounded man's knee. "It went clean through. When he stops the bleeding you'll be okay."

Ben eased back into his position as the man's jacket was removed, a difficult task with them all lying down. The man gritted his teeth against the pain.

"We just lay here," George Toussaint said. "They gone keep shootin' and pick us off one by one."

Ben was all too aware of that. He had no answer for Toussaint, though. His mind worked feverishly to think of a plan to get them out of the trap the robbers had sprung.

As if to underscore their predicament, there was a volley of shots from the road ahead of them where the other three gunmen were concealed. The robbers' strategy was clear to

Ben now; they would alternate shooting from each position. Those not shooting would move forward while Ben and his men were distracted by the shooting, moving ever closer. It was just a matter of time until one group or the other was in a position to get clear shots them.

He couldn't maintain the position for long.

"You're right, George," he said. "We need to take the fight to them somehow."

Toussaint's dark face lit up in a smile. The man relished a good fight.

"What you got in mind?" he asked.

Ben explained what he thought the robbers were doing, and suggested using a variant of it themselves. The three men who'd circled around them were closest, and therefore, the most dangerous. His plan was relatively simple. While the rest of the group would lay down a volley of heavy fire at both groups of robbers, four troopers, Davis, Tatum, Hightower, and Buckley, the best shots besides Ben and Toussaint, would slip out of the barricade and work downslope through the scrub and make their way up the trail toward the three, who, if things worked, would have their heads down to keep out of range of the withering fire.

"It might work," Hightower said. The other three nodded agreement.

As the four men eased to the side, preparing

to crawl underneath the wagon and into the brush, Ben repositioned the remainder of the group to have an equal number of weapons firing in each direction.

"Get ready," he said quietly. He looked at Hightower, who would be the first to go. Hightower nodded. "Fire," Ben yelled.

The crash of eleven rifles firing almost simultaneously was deafening. A cloud of gun smoke hung over the wagons, causing Ben and the others to cough. But, between coughs, he ordered them to continue firing.

It worked; no return fire came from either direction.

While part of his mind focused on reloading and firing his carbine, another part was counting off seconds since the four troopers had slipped from the relative safety of the wagons. Ben knew that Hightower, with the skills he'd learned when he and his mother had lived with the Indians that had kidnapped them, would be able to move quickly and quietly through the brush. The others wouldn't be as quick or quiet, but each had experience in the field and would follow Hightower's lead.

"Cease fire," he said, when he felt the four men had had enough time to get well away.

The sudden quiet was as deafening as the gunfire had been.

"Think we hit anybody?" Danford asked.

"Probably not," Ben replied. "But, the idea was just to keep their heads down, and we did that."

"What do we do now?"

Ben gave the man a sympathetic look.

"We wait a few more minutes to see what they do next."

The crestfallen look on Danford's face told Ben that this wasn't what he'd been expecting, wanting to hear, but it would have to do. He looked over at the wounded trooper who seemed to be okay. His tunic had been removed and his shirt torn away so that a bandage could be wound around his shoulder. The bandage was bloodstained, but there was no sign of seepage, indicating that the bleeding had stopped. One less thing to worry about, Ben thought.

"You feeling better?" He asked the man.

"It hurt like the devil," the man said, wincing. "But, I think I gone live."

"Next time, stay down."

"That for sure." The wounded soldier smiled weakly.

The sound of gunfire caused Ben's head to whip around. It came from the direction of the three gunmen. He recognized the unmistakable crack of the Springfield carbine along with what he suspected was a Winchester repeater; Hightower and the others had encountered the outlaws.

The fire kept up for about two minutes and then as quickly as it had started it stopped.

For Ben, the next few minutes were the longest of his life. Had Hightower and the others been able to prevail, or had he sent four men to their deaths? This was one aspect of command he'd never learned to view dispassionately, this possibility that his decisions could cause the death of his friends. Just when he thought he couldn't take the waiting any longer, a figure appeared on the trail. He could see that the man coming over the curve of the slight hill wore a cavalry uniform, so he began to breathe easier. Then, he recognized Hightower's lanky form when he raised his carbine high above his head and waved it. The mission had been a success.

Ben crawled toward the opening between the two wagons and began waving toward Hightower. First he pointed to his rear, and then he made a sweeping motion to the left. Hightower waved and disappeared over the hill.

Toussaint chuckled.

"So, you gone use they trick right back at 'em, huh?"

Ben smiled.

"What's good for the goose is good for the gander, my pa always says."

Ben rearranged the men, leaving only two to cover the east side, while moving the rest to aim west toward the remaining five outlaws.

"W-what are you planning to do, sergeant?" Danford asked when Ben returned to his position under the settler's wagon.

Ben moved to a position on his back, with his shoulders against the packs, so that he could see everyone.

"Marcus, Hezekiah, Tom, and Lucas are coming with me," he said. "We'll ease out front here, grab our horses and ride off toward the southeast to get out of range. Then we'll turn around and head back along the bottom of that ridgeline south of us until we've flanked the outlaws. That way, we'll have 'em in a crossfire from Samuel and the others. If you fellas down here see one of 'em pop his head up, take a shot as well."

The four men Ben had named to accompany him nodded, slight smiles creasing their faces. Toussaint, however, frowned deeply.

"Shouldn't I be the one to lead this, Ben?" he asked quietly. "You in charge of the whole shebang, so you oughta stay here where you can watch everything, you know."

Ben and George Toussaint hadn't exactly hit it off when they first met, but over the many months they'd served together, had developed a close friendship. He also knew that it would have been tactically sound to put his second in command in charge of the little foray he was planning, but he had to occasionally demonstrate to the men that he wasn't sending them out to do anything he wasn't prepared to do himself.

"I'm tired of layin' here on my backside," Ben said. "I'm leaving you in charge here and getting out to stretch my legs." He smiled broadly. He lifted the canvas bag and tossed it to Toussaint. "Keep hold of that until I get back."

He didn't have to say, "and, if I don't get back, it's your responsibility to get these two bags to the adjutant;" the look in his friend's eyes told him the message was received and understood.

"Okay," Toussaint said. "We'll provide cover fire when you ready to slip out."

Ben and the others checked their weapons and ammunition.

"You ready?" he asked them. They nodded. "Okay then, let's move out."

As they wormed their way to the horses, dragging their saddles, Toussaint and the others took aim at the rise to the west and began firing methodically. There was no return fire.

They kept as low as possible as they saddled their horses. When they were done, they took the reins and moved east along the trail a ways and then to the south into the tall scrub. Once they were about a hundred yards deep into the grass, they mounted and began moving at a trot southwest to make their way to a point somewhat south of where they figured the outlaws were.

The firing from their position kept up. Ben knew that Toussaint understood what he was trying to do, and was doing what he could to keep the outlaws distracted.

When they'd reached a point that Ben estimated was directly south of the top of the rise, Ben had them ride a bit further west in hopes they would come out behind the outlaws. At they swung north, he heard the crack of rifle fire from somewhere to his front; Hightower and the others must have arrived and engaged the outlaws, he thought. He spurred his horse to a gallop and pulled his carbine from the scabbard. The other four followed suit.

As they burst from the tall grass onto the trail, he saw that they had indeed worked their way past the outlaws who were now moving toward their horses, firing as they ran. He could hear the crack of carbines and see puffs of smoke from a clump of trees to the northeast.

"Let 'em have it, fellas," he yelled as he brought his carbine to his shoulder and fired one-handed.

Taking fire from two sides, the five outlaws panicked. They were now scrambling madly toward their horses. The animals, picking up the fear from their owners, were bucking and shying, trying to pull free from the small bushes they'd been tethered to. The outlaws were firing back over their shoulders as they ran, but their shots went wild.

Ben, on the other hand, was calmly aiming, and as the carbine bucked against his shoulder, one of the outlaws threw his hands in the air and pitched forward. He twitched once and was still, face down in the dirt. Another screamed and dropped to his knees, grabbing at his right leg, where a large dark stain was spreading along his trouser leg.

The three outlaws in front, ignoring their comrade's cries for help, leapt for their horses, ripping the reins from the bushes. Lying low across the horses' shoulders, they kicked them into action, all attempts to fire back at the cavalrymen forgotten in their desire to get as far away from them as possible.

Hightower got to the wounded outlaw just before Ben did. The man was sitting on the ground, his hands clasped around his thigh, moaning as he rocked back and forth.

"Ow, it hurt," he cried. He looked up at Hightower, fear in his eyes. "Please don't shoot me."

Both Hightower and Ben regarded him impassively. Ben walked over and kicked the man's rifle away. He then reached down and removed the pistol from the man's holster.

"Patch him up as best you can, Samuel," Ben said. "Then tie him up and put him in one of the wagons. We'll take him back to the fort and let the colonel decide what to do with him."

"What about the dead ones?" Hightower asked. "This one here and the three at the other end of the trail."

Ben took a deep breath and shrugged.

"Guess we ought to bury 'em."

Charles Ray

6.

After burying the four dead outlaws and retrieving their five horses, which Ben had tethered to the lead wagon, they put the wounded man in the second wagon with the wounded trooper. He'd recovered from the shock of being shot and sat with his back against the seat with a carbine aimed at the wounded outlaw's gut. The man, though in pain, kept his lips clenched tight, and his eyes stayed glued on the barrel of the carbine pointed at him.

It was late afternoon when they reached Danford's place, little more than a mid-sized adobe hut, barn and corral, set a few hundred yards off the trail on a broad grassy plain. A stream cut across the property from west to east. Near the house, Ben could see an area of plowed ground where Danford grew vegetables for his family. Two milk cows grazed near the barn, and several horses grazed some distance away. It wasn't prosperous, but the way the man's chest swelled as they approached, it was clear that he was proud of it.

"You're welcome to stop and rest a spell," Danford said as Ben rode back to where he'd stopped his wagon.

"Thank you kindly," Ben said, saluting the man by touching two fingers to the brim of his campaign hat. "But, I reckon we'd best be moving on so we aren't overdue at the fort. Wouldn't want 'em to worry."

"I got me a feelin' them folk up at the fort ain't too worried 'bout you, sergeant." Danford reached a hand down. He and Ben shook. "It 'pears to me you just about the toughest soldier they got."

"Just about everybody in the Ninth is tough," Ben said. "Our motto is 'We can: We will', and that means we never give up, even when the going gets tough."

"I reckon they's some people back in Santa Fe know the meanin' of that right 'bout now. Well, sergeant, hope the rest of your journey is peaceful . . . and . . . I want to thank you for lettin' me ride along with you."

Ben inclined his head, accepting the thanks. He didn't say that had he not allowed Danford to accompany them, the surviving robbers would likely have fallen on him in their frustration at failing to rob the cavalry convoy.

He felt relief at having protected the man from danger, and he felt pride at having brought his own unit through with only one injury.

"You take care, sir," Ben said. He nudged his horse aside to allow Danford to pull his wagon out of line and head down the narrow trail toward his house.

As the wagon neared the house, Ben saw the door flung open and two children, scrawny little girls wearing identical gingham dresses came running out, making a dash toward the oncoming wagon. They were followed by a tall, broad-shouldered woman with long blonde hair who was hugely pregnant. She stopped just outside the door.

Danford stopped the wagon and jumped down. The two girls swarmed him. He hoisted them one by one up to the seat of the wagon and climbed up behind him. When he'd pulled it close to the house, he hopped down again, and took the woman in his arms while the girls clung to his legs.

As Ben watched, the woman pulled away from her husband and looked his way. She waved at him. The two girls also waved. Even from the distance, Ben could see the woman's shoulders were shaking. He imagined he could see the tears that would be streaming down her cheeks. For the children, Danford's story would be just a great adventure, but Ben knew it would be different for his wife. Yet again, she'd had to endure nights of waiting, wondering if he'd make it home alive. Well, thanks to the men of the Ninth Cavalry, he'd made it this time.

Ben waved back.

Here was at least one settler family that had a good opinion of the dusky soldiers of the Ninth. Far too many out here on the frontier disliked the black soldiers almost as much as they hated the Indians. It never seemed to matter that the cavalrymen risked their lives every day to keep the land safe for them; they couldn't get past their prejudices and hatred. Sometimes for Ben this battle was tougher than fighting renegade Indians or outlaws.

He sighed and waved once more. Then, he wheeled his horse around to face the waiting men of the convoy.

"Okay," he said. "Let's get a move on. We've got to get this mail to the fort."

7.

Ben didn't allow a stop until it was nearly dark and they were several miles northeast of the Danford place. After their encounter with the outlaws, no one complained when he had the wagons put in a defensive formation with the horses inside, and insisted on four sentries, two each east and west of the camp site.

The next day, he roused the men at first light, and after a quick breakfast set out. They made Las Vegas by late afternoon. Ben put the wagons and horses, along with their prisoner, in a livery stable at the north end of the town and assigned four guards standing four-hour shifts. He took the two canvas bags with him to the room he got in a seedy hotel not far from the stable.

On the following morning, with only around 45 miles left until they reached Fort Union, Ben let the men sleep until sunrise before rousing them. After a quick meal in the hotel's tiny dining room, they set out. Without the settler's wagon to slow them, he was able to set a fast pace, enabling them to pull through the main gate of the fort just before sunset.

The prisoner was turned over to the sergeant of the guard who had him escorted under armed escort to the fort's hospital for treatment. When the doctor cleared it, he would be transferred to a cell in the fort stockade. The wounded trooper walked to the hospital under his own power. The mail was delivered to the mail room where it was secured for the night, and Ben delivered the two bags of cash to the adjutant, who took it with an expression of relief when Ben told him of the robbery attempt.

After the adjutant dismissed him, Ben went to the barracks where he ate a light meal, washed his face, stripped off his dark blue jacket and light blue pants, and dressed only in his cotton shirt and underpants, dropped into his bed and instantly into a deep sleep.

Ben's eyes snapped open. The first thing he noticed was the brightness of the light in the barracks. The next was Malachi Davis's round brown face covered in a huge smile hovering over him.

"Mornin', Ben," Davis said. "How'd you sleep?"

"Hmph, uh, what time is it?" Ben asked.

"Oh, I reckon it must be near eight."

"You fellas let me sleep through reveille?" Ben growled as he sat up, flinging aside the blanket that he didn't remember crawling under.

Davis's smile disappeared to be replaced by a look of worry.

"Uh, well, you was so tuckered out, George said to let you sleep. Troop commander said it was okay too. Fact of matter, he done give the whole detachment the mornin' off."

Ben shook his head to clear the cobwebs. As his mind came more fully awake, his expression softened.

"Okay, I guess." Ben rubbed the stubble on his cheek. His stomach growled. "But, I missed breakfast, and it's a long time till noon mess call."

Davis's face brightened again.

"I done thought of that," he said. "I brung you some biscuits, sausage and gravy, and a bit of coffee to wash it down."

He put a plate and cup on the box beside Ben's bed. Steam drifted upward from the cup carrying the rich aroma of freshly brewed coffee.

Ben would have preferred brushing his teeth before eating, but the growling of his stomach and the hollow feeling were overpowering. He grabbed a sausage, still warm, and stuffed it into his mouth, followed by a bite from one of the large biscuits after dipping it in the thick gravy. Even mixed with the sour taste of sleep it was delicious. He washed it down with a long gulp from the cup. In minutes there was only a chunk of biscuit and a small dot of gravy left on the plate, which he quickly demolished.

"Um, I really needed that. Thanks, Malachi."

"Thought you'd like it," Davis said. "Now that you done ate, the major said he want to see you."

Of course he would, Ben thought. Wainwright would want a fuller report of events than Ben had given when they arrived the day before.

"Soon's I clean up I'll go see him," he said.

After brushing his teeth, shaving and taking a quick bath in lukewarm water, Ben put on a new uniform. With his campaign hat at a rakish angle and his knee-high boots freshly polished, he reported to Major Wainwright in the troop headquarters building.

"I hope you're well rested, sergeant," the officer said when Ben snapped to attention and saluted in front of the large crate he used for a desk.

"Yes, sir," Ben replied. "Sorry I overslept and missed first call."

Wainwright casually saluted and waved Ben to another smaller crate at the side of his 'desk.'

"No problem with that. You and your men deserved some rest after what you went through. Now, before we go over to the hospital and question the prisoner you brought in, tell me exactly what happened."

Ben gave a precise, detailed account of events from their departure from Santa Fe. When he mentioned the settler he'd allowed to accompany the convoy, Wainwright frowned slightly, but then nodded for Ben to continue. Ben's description of the fight with the outlaws brought a smile to the major's face.

"You and your men acquitted yourselves well," Wainwright said when Ben had finished. "That maneuver to outflank the robbers was particularly impressive. I'll be sending a letter of commendation to regiment for your file. Now, let's go see what our prisoner has to say."

Ben walked on Wainwright's left as they made their way to the northeast quadrant of the fort to the hospital. Except for a couple of troopers getting bandages put on cuts they'd suffered in the carpenter shop, the hospital had only one other patient, the wounded outlaw. He'd been put in one of the two-man rooms. Two troopers armed with carbines guarded the door. The men snapped to attention and saluted when Ben and the major approached.

The outlaw was sitting up on the bed, still wearing his regular clothing, but with the cloth of the pants of his injured leg had been cut away. The wound was swathed in clean bandages. His face darkened in a wary frown when Ben and Wainwright entered.

The hospital orderlies had cleaned the area around the wound so that it could be treated, but hadn't bathed the patient. The rank smell of sweat hung heavy in the air along with the antiseptics the doctor had used in cleaning the wound.

Wainwright went to one side of the bed while Ben moved to the other. The man's head pivoted from side to side, watching them both. There was a slight flicker of defiance in his gaze, but the dominant emotion was fear.

"I ain't no soldier," he said weakly. "Ya'll got no call keepin' me here."

"Well now," Wainwright said. "You attacked a cavalry unit, so there's some question about that. Of course, what we'll likely do is turn you over to the sheriff down in Las Vegas for trial. You're lucky none of my men were killed, so they aren't likely to hang you. But, you will spend a long time in the territorial prison."

The man's eyes narrowed, and he laughed.

"You think a court out here's gone accept the word of a colored, even a soldier, against a white man? You gone ahead and do that."

Wainwright looked at Ben, his right eyebrow raised. His thin lips curled in a half smile.

"Yeah," Ben said. "But, they might just take the word of the white settler who was with us, and saw it all." He returned Wainwright's smile. "In face, major, I think we ought to take this fella back to Santa Fe to stand trial. I expect folks there know him."

The outlaw's face paled. Whether it was at the news of the settler being a witness, or the prospect of being sent back to Santa Fe, he was clearly unsettled.

"L-look, ain't no call for that," he said weakly. "No need to be sendin' me to Santa Fe."

Wainwright stared down at the man, not a trace of compassion on his suntanned face.

"Can you give me one good reason I shouldn't?" he said coldly.

The man looked pleadingly from Ben to Wainwright, and back to Ben. Ben didn't know why, but the he came to the conclusion that what the man feared most was going back to

Santa Fe.

"Why did you try to rob mail wagons in the first place?" Ben asked.

"We didn't want the mail," the man said. "We was after the payroll money you was carryin'."

"How'd you know about the money? The man at the depot didn't even tell me until the mornin' he gave it to me."

"They's somebody in the depot told us," the man said.

"One of the clerks? Who?" Wainwright asked.

"I don't know. Zeke, he was the head of our gang, he knew; but, your soldiers done kilt him."

"That's not much," the major said. He had a worried look on his face.

"B-but," the outlaw said. "It's all I know. Y'all ain't gone send me back to Santa Fe, is you? You send me back there, they kill me for sure."

Wainwright was staring off into the middle distance like a man in a daydream.

"Uh, major," Ben said. "What are we going to do with him?"

Wainwright continued to stare at something Ben couldn't see; then, he shook himself.

"I guess we ought to turn him over to the authorities in Las Vegas," he said. "Let them take care of it. I'll have the sergeant major get a detail together as soon as he's able to be moved."

"My detachment could do it, sir," Ben offered.

"No, sergeant; you and your men have done enough. You've got a day off coming, so go on and enjoy it. I have a light duty for you tomorrow; hopefully one that won't involve getting shot at."

Wainwright smiled weakly at his own attempt at humor. Ben didn't find it funny.

8.

It had been so long since Ben had had an honest off day, he was at first at a loss as to what to do with his time. He cleaned his equipment, but that task only took an hour. He didn't relish just sitting around the barracks; nor did he want to visit the tent city just outside the fort's gates where black, white, and Mexican women of easy virtue lurked waiting to part the troopers from their money, gamblers sat smiling as they shuffled marked cards, and purveyors of all manner of alcoholic beverages, each more vile than the one before, tried to tempt soldiers to 'just try a sip.'

Unlike many of the men, who had been mostly illiterate when they joined the cavalry, Ben could read and write, and was pretty fair with figures, so he really had no excuse to go to the fort chapel and visit with the chaplain whose duty on Sunday was to try and save the men's souls, but who spent the other six days of the week trying to teach them to read and write at a basic level. Also unlike most of the others, Ben, while he wasn't atheist, had some problems with the idea of a just God who would let a people be enslaved and abused. He'd felt that way even as a child, but had never expressed it to anyone. He just avoided churches and preachers.

As he walked from the hospital toward his barracks, he heard music coming from the vicinity of a building to the south of the hospital and not far from the chapel. It sounded like music being played for a parade. Ben was curious, so he followed the sound. He rounded the small building, where he found seventeen troopers, dressed only in light blue trousers and cotton undershirts, gathered under a large tree. They were holding musical instruments, horns and drums, and were playing a marching tune under the watchful eye of a dark-skinned sergeant major waving a baton in time with the music.

The band, Ben knew, had just returned to Fort Union after a tour of the other forts in the territory where units of the Ninth were stationed. He'd heard that there was pressure to assign the band to Fort Marcy near Santa Fe because the regimental headquarters was there, and the town was the territorial capital. This move had been resisted, however, because there were no troops at Fort Marcy. The men at the forts scattered around the territory enjoyed the band's performances, as did many of the settlers in the small towns. Despite the prejudice the white settlers had against black soldiers, the band was almost always welcomed to participate in local celebrations.

Ben stopped under the shade of a small tree, some twenty yards from the band. He just stood there listening as they played "I've Been Working on the Railroad,' a song he remembered the black field workers back home in East Texas singing from time to time as they picked cotton for one of the white farmers. The men, and not a few women and children, worked from sunup to sundown, and though they were no longer slaves, the pittance they were paid for their back-breaking labor was barely enough to buy a meal in the few local taverns that would serve blacks.

The harmony of the music was nice, but as the words flooded into Ben's mind, *I've been workin' on de railroad, all the livelong day, I've been workin' on de railroad, jest to pass the time away,* he felt an unmeasurable sadness. He wondered how many of the men playing the song so beautifully were reminded of the toil and pain their music evoked.

He could understand how the singing of these songs, no matter how popular they were with the men and local settlers, no matter how masterfully they were played and sung, could make George Toussaint angry.

He walked slowly, but purposefully, past the musicians, who paid no heed to his passing, heading further south to the large athletic field in the southeast quadrant. In the distance he could see several men running around the area.

As he got closer, he could see that it was the Fort Union baseball team, a group of the more athletic soldiers from the unit stationed at the post. They were broken down into two teams of nine each, practicing against each other for one of the many competitions they played in around the area against teams from other forts or from the local communities.

Ben enjoyed watching the game, although he'd never played himself. Baseball was one of the most popular sports among the soldiers of the Ninth. A game that had its origins in the English games of Rounders and Cricket, it had been played in America since the earliest days. But, it wasn't until 1845, when Alexander Joy Cartwright, a volunteer fireman and bank clerk in New York created a set of rules that distinguished it from its English forebears that it had become a truly American game. Ben knew that there were baseball teams back east that played against each other in organized competitions, but they were restricted to white players. In some communities where there were enough black men, all-black teams were formed and played against each other. Out here on the western frontier, though, despite the prejudice white settlers had against the dark-skinned soldiers of the cavalry and infantry who protected them, they often allowed them to play against local teams.

The players practiced under the watchful eye of a young white lieutenant who was obviously the team's coach. Five other soldiers, dressed like the players in just their uniform pants and beige undershirts, stood along the edges of the field cheering for one team or the other.

As Ben approached the field, the young lieutenant came over to him.

"You come to try out for the team, sergeant?" he asked.

Ben snapped to attention and saluted the officer.

"No, sir," he said. "I just thought I'd watch for a while if that's okay?"

The lieutenant looked Ben up and down. He reached up and squeezed his bicep.

"Sure, soldier, you can watch. But, you

ought to think about playing. You got the build of a good baseball player; strong shoulders, long arms and legs; and you look like you might be good at the game."

"Uh, no sir; I've never played. I just like watching."

"I've seen you around, sergeant," the officer said. "Have you been in the Ninth long?"

"Yes, sir," Ben said. "I'm Sergeant Ben Carter. I came from Texas with the Ninth."

The lieutenant's eyes widened.

"Sergeant Carter? So, you're the one the colonel and major are always talking about. I didn't know you hung around the fort."

Ben smiled. The officer's expression was a mixture of disbelief and awe. The game had stopped, and the players were all staring at Ben. Dang, he thought, I didn't know I had a reputation. He stood a little taller.

"I don't usually, sir. Major Wainwright decided to give me and my men some easy duty for a while. We were out in the field a long time."

"Word is the last duty wasn't all that easy. You had to fight off outlaws getting the payroll back here."

Ben nodded.

"That was some maneuver you pulled, according to the major. They didn't teach us that kind of tactics back at West Point."

Ben wanted to say that the instructors at the military academy had learned their soldiering from books, while he'd learned his by surviving against hostile Indians and outlaws. He'd also learned that insulting the white officers of the unit wasn't good sense. This one seemed okay, but some of them barely tolerated the presence of black soldiers; anything they saw as insulting or insubordination brought terrible consequences for the offender.

"No, sir, I guess they don't. It just seemed like the thing to do at the time," Ben said with as much modesty as he could muster.

"Well, by damn, sergeant, it worked." The tone in the officer's voice was definitely respect, and it made Ben's chest swell. "Well, sergeant, you watch all you want, and if you change your mind about joining the team, you just let me know." He turned back to the staring men. "All right, who told you men to stop practicing? Get back to work. We got a game against the ranchers down in Las Vegas in two days, so we have to be ready."

The lieutenant became the harsh coach in an instant. Quickly, Ben's presence was forgotten. He moved off by himself and watched them play for a few minutes, enjoying it, but not really understanding the finer points of the game.

No one noticed when he wandered away.

Since it was getting on to mid-day, Ben walked to the mess near his barracks, where he found most of his men already sitting at a table in the corner eating. He noticed that the other men, while they would give the men of the detachment glances as they passed, didn't sit with them.

The meal consisted of pork chops, collard greens and corn pone. Ben only took a modest amount.

"What you been doin' all mornin?" Toussaint asked as Ben flopped into a chair across the table from him.

"Not much. Just walkin' around the fort."

"Borin', ain't it? It's like sittin' watchin' a caterpillar crawl up a leaf."

Heads nodded around the table.

"Yeah," Malachi Davis said. "And, you notice how nobody else wants to have much to do with us?"

"That's because we don't spend much time here, and most of the men don't know us," Ben said. "I did get asked to join the baseball team this morning."

All eyes were on him, mouths open in astonishment.

Finally, young Davis broke the silence. "You gone do it; join the baseball team?"

Ben laughed.

"Of course not; I don't know how to play baseball. I do like to watch, but watching and playing are different."

"That was nice of 'em to ask you, though," Davis said.

"So," Marcus Scott said from the end of the table opposite Ben. "What we suppose to do with ourselves for the rest of the day? I done cleaned my gear twice, and 'cept for a rip in my shelter tent half, other than goin' to quartermaster this afternoon and gettin' a new one, I ain't got nothin' to do."

Ben sympathized with him. If you didn't play a musical instrument, sport, or like slipping off the base to go to the tent city, there wasn't much to occupy the mind of a soldier not on a work detail.

"I suppose," he said. "You could try reading. That's what I plan to do."

Samuel Hightower nodded, but Scott

snarled.

"Readin'? You mean set somewhere with my face buried in a book. Naw, readin' gives me headaches."

"That's 'cause you don't know how to read," Tom Holman said. "You git headaches from your lips movin' so much."

"I do too know how to read," Scott protested. "And, I can cipher too."

"Yeah, you can count to twenty long's you take your boots off first."

This caused everyone at the table, Scott included, to double over with laughter, which drew stares from nearby tables. While it was just good natured banter, Ben knew it could escalate to a full-blown argument if the men were forced to remain idle for much longer.

"I hear the new chaplain's holdin' a readin' class today. Maybe you could drop in and offer to help him out."

Scott nodded, his eyes narrowed in concentration. "Yeah, reckon I could do that. You want to join me, Tom?"

"Might's well; nothin' else to do."

The rest of the meal went quietly. Afterwards, Ben went back to his barracks. He reached under his bed for the box in which he kept his books and magazines, yellowed and dog-eared with age. He pulled out an old back issue of *Atlantic* magazine, a much read publication. Some of the officers had subscriptions, and when they finished reading issues would give them to Ben on occasion. He liked thumbing through page after page of gray type, pausing over unfamiliar words or phrases until he could figure out their meaning from context.

In this issue, there was a story written by William Dean Howells, 'The Lady of Aroostook,' about Lydia Blood, a 19-year-old orphan traveling by ship from America to Italy to live with relatives. The story had been broken up in parts, and printed in different issues of the magazine, so Ben had missed some of it. But, the parts he'd been able to read fascinated him, with descriptions of people and places such as he'd never seen before. To him, born in the swamplands of East Texas and spending his life there and on the high plains and deserts of West Texas and New Mexico Territory, the Eastern United States was like an exotic foreign country.

Someday, he thought as he read the story, *I'm going to see some of that other world out there. A world where the streets are more than rivers of mud when it rains, with toilets inside the house, and where you don't have to worry about Indians or outlaws every time you go outside.*

Charles Ray

9.

Friday morning, when the adjutant stopped Ben on the way to mess and told him that he and his detachment were to guard another wood cutting detail, he felt a sense of relief. As boring as that duty had been, it was preferable to being stuck on the fort with nothing to do.

At breakfast, the men of the detachment reacted the same way. They were so happy at the prospect of getting off the base; they ignored the nature of the assignment.

That nature hit them squarely in the face when they rode up to the main gate to meet the work detail they were to escort.

Four of the larger wagons, each pulled by a team of four horses, were lined up at the gate. Each wagon had a driver and four troopers on it, and while each trooper was armed with the regulation carbine and revolver, they also had axes, large saws, other metal tools, and several lengths of rope.

"That's a lot of tools you got just for cuttin' kindlin'," Toussaint said to the sergeant on the first wagon as he rode up.

The man turned and spit a gob of brown juice at the ground beside the wagon and smiled at Toussaint. His teeth, the few he had left, were stained brown.

"Who done tole you we'se cuttin' kindlin', friend? We ain't cuttin' no kindlin'; we'se got to cut some big logs so's they kin build a 'stension on the stable, and fix up the quartermaster roof."

Toussaint's dark brows rose in query, and he turned to Ben. Ben shrugged.

"So, I imagine this job will take more than one day," Ben said.

"Got that right," the sergeant said, spitting again. "Reckon we'se gone be back here Monday or Tuesday. We'se got to cut the trees and do some trimmin' and dressin' fo we can put 'em in the wagons."

Ben cursed himself for not asking for more detail. He hadn't prepared his detachment adequately for the mission.

"Okay," he said. "We'll have to wait until

my men draw four days' rations." He turned to Toussaint. "George, you mind drawin' mine? I need to find out from the sergeant here more about this work detail."

Ben didn't have to add that the men also needed to bring along their tent halves; everyone had heard the sergeant's response.

It took half an hour for the detachment to secure the rations and gear needed for an extended stay in the field. This was something to which they were accustomed, having done it so much in the past. Ben learned that the men on the wood cutting detail had each been selected because of experience as lumberjacks or workers in lumber mills as civilians, and the sergeant assured him they would work as fast as safety allowed, but that cutting down the size trees they had to cut wasn't something you could rush. In his mind, Ben revised the estimate of their stay in the field upwards by two days and hoped that the others would take the same view.

The sun was well up by the time they headed northwest from the fort, toward the thick forests of the Sangre de Cristo foothills. They made it to their destination, a thick stand of hardwoods and evergreens about twenty miles from the fort, by noon. Ben put four men of his detachment on guard and had the rest help the woodcutters set up camp.

He had the wagons arranged in a modified version of the defensive maneuver he'd used with the mail wagons; arranged in a square, but with space between them so two men could ride abreast. The weapons and gear were placed inside the square along with the sleep tents and fire. The horses were tethered at one corner on the side nearest the mountains to their west.

The woodcutters looked dubious and shook their heads at this arrangement until Marcus Scott reminded them that just such an arrangement had saved their lives when they were attacked by outlaws on their journey from Santa Fe. Such was the reputation of Ben and his men, this shut off any more doubts.

After finishing the noon meal, the woodcutters went into the trees to their northwest and started marking trees for cutting. Ben left two men to guard the camp and had the rest mounted to patrol around the area where the cutters were working. Not that he expected any trouble, but it was good to keep field discipline, and in truth, he and the others liked being in the saddle.

Ben rode a wide circle around the area, never so far that he couldn't hear the sounds of the woodcutters working, satisfying himself that there were no immediate threats.

During the afternoon, the few wispy clouds that had been in the dark blue sky in the morning had evaporated and the temperature rose high enough to cause many of the men to remove their shirts, exposing their dark brown and bronze upper bodies that quickly became shiny with sweat. The sound of axes, making a 'thunking' noise as they were slammed into trunks to notch selected trees to control the direction of fall, the rasp of the big two-man saws as they cut through the trunk, and finally, the loud snap as the last ligament of trunk broke followed by a crashing sound as the trees toppled filled the air. When the first trees fell, the forest erupted with birds of all types taking flight in fright, and small animals like rabbits and squirrels scurrying to get as far away from these two-legged invaders as possible. On a distant ridge, Ben saw a family of elk, standing majestically gazing down at the forest as if curious about the source of this disturbance in their normally tranquil home.

The woodcutters stopped work an hour before sunset and made their way back to camp. Ben was standing by the fire sipping coffee from his cup. When the first man passed him, the odor from the man's sweaty body almost caused Ben to drop the cup.

"Whoa, friend," he said. "Ain't you gonna

take a bath?"

The man sniffed at his underarms and gave Ben a querying look.

"Where I gone do that? You see a bathtub 'round here anywhere?"

Ben pulled his red scarf over his nose and backed away from the man.

"There's a stream just over yonder in that stand of pine trees," he said. "I saw it when I was riding around. You go on over there and wash the sweat and smell off before you come in here." He glared at the other woodcutters who were standing just outside the perimeter of the four wagons. "That goes for all of you. I'm not having you stink up the camp site. Malachi, show 'em where the stream is, and give 'em some of that soap from your saddle bag."

Davis nodded and retrieved a large brick of white from his bag. He tossed it to the nearest woodcutter, keeping well upwind of the man.

"Y'all follow me," he said, and stepped quickly around the men heading for the copse of trees.

As Ben watched the men walk away, he decided that it would be wise to lead by example. He briskly strode after them, breathing shallowly to minimize the acrid reek of their bodies. When they arrived at the stream, he led the way by shucking his clothes and, taking the bar of soap from one of the woodcutters, waded into the stream.

The water was frigid at first, but the longer he stayed submerged, the more comfortable it became. He lathered his body from top to bottom and then ducked to rinse. When he felt a hand on his shoulder, he turned to find one of the woodcutters, a medium brown skinned man with tightly curled reddish hair, standing next to him.

"Kin I borrow the soap, sergeant?" the man asked.

All of the other woodcutters were standing hip deep in the stream shivering as well, waiting their turn at the bar of soap.

Seeing Ben in the water, the men of his detachment took turns bathing. When everyone, including the old tobacco chewing sergeant, had bathed and put their clothing back on, they returned to the camp. The smell of the lye-based soap settled in Ben's nostrils, a vast improvement over stale sweat. The smiles and glowing faces around the cook fire as they waited for the beans in the big iron pot to warm told him that everyone shared this thought.

The next morning, the woodcutters ate breakfast at sunrise and were soon back in the forest, hacking and sawing. Ben left Holman and Scott at the camp, and along with the rest of the detachment, spent the morning scouting the area. It was as peaceful as the day before had been – until just before noon.

Ben had just ridden past the spring, not far from where they'd bathed the evening before, and was nearing the wagons, when he heard a scream. At first, it sounded like an animal, but when it pierced the air a second time, he could tell it was a human. He urged his horse in the direction of the sound.

When the scream sounded a third time, the sound of axes and saws stopped, and voices started yelling in the forest. The screaming, accompanied by the sound of something or someone crashing through the undergrowth, seemed to be getting nearer.

Ben pulled his horse to a halt. Best to wait and see what's happening, he thought.

Three figures appeared among the trees where the forest began to thin out, running toward the clearing as if their lives depended on it, and screaming like they were being pursued by demons. And then, Ben saw that they were being pursued, not be demons, but almost as bad.

A bull elk, fully six feet tall at the shoulders with a large rack of horns, ten or twelve razor-sharp tines at the end, extending out four feet from its head, came charging out of the trees, its head lowered, the sharp points of its horns aimed at the retreating hindquarters of the fleeing soldiers. The elk was some twenty yards or so back, but closing. The men ran as fast as their legs could carry them, and for a moment it appeared they might make the safety of the camp. But, one man's foot caught on something and he fell forward like one of the trees he'd been cutting, the wind knocked out of him. The elk slowed, saw the helpless man on the ground, lowered its horns and resumed its charge.

There was no question of the other two men turning and helping their companion, even if they'd been aware of his predicament. Their only thought was to make it to the safety of the wagons.

Ben pulled his carbine from the scabbard. He shoved a cartridge into the chamber. The elk was not about twenty feet from the dazed man. Ben put the butt of the rifle to his shoulder and took aim. The elk was not at ten feet and closing, the horns nearly raking the ground. Just as the animal was about six feet from its target, Ben squeezed the trigger.

The carbine bucked against his shoulder. The elk bucked and dropped its head, its weight causing it to slide forward another three feet, and then it stopped dead, figuratively and literally. Ben's shot had pierced the left front chest, tearing through the bull's heart, killing it almost instantly. It toppled to the side, the deadly tines of its rack just inches from the now reviving man's boots.

When the man looked back and saw how close he'd come to being skewered, he fainted.

10.

Ben had the others haul the unconscious soldier and the elk carcass to the camp. While they waited for him to regain consciousness, his two companions explained what had happened.

The three had just felled a large pine tree, and were in the process of trimming it for transport, when a cow elk and two calves; or, as one of the men put it, 'a big mammy deer and her two babies,' came out of the trees about thirty feet from where they were working. Southerners who had never seen anything larger than a white tail deer, they were mesmerized by the sight, and dropped what they were doing to move closer to the three animals.

"They sho nuff looked peaceable enough,"

one said. "I thought we'd jest pet the little ones, you know."

To their surprise, instead of fleeing as the deer they knew would have done, the cow lowered her head and put herself between them and the calves, making snorting noises. If the men had been smarter, or more experienced in the ways of the animals of the west, they would have immediately withdrawn. But, they thought this was cute, and started teasing the cow, which only caused her to snort louder.

A crashing in the bush behind the cow and calves told them why the cow was making the noises she made – she'd been calling for help. A bull, the largest 'deer' the men had ever seen, snorting and bellowing, broke through the bush and, spotting the three two-legged creatures tormenting his cow and calves, charged.

"Wasn't nothin' peaceable 'bout that monster," the other man said. "He's wantin' to stick them horns on his head in us."

"So, we jest naturally lit out fast as we could," the first man said. "Iffen you hadn't been here, he'd likely got us too."

Ben wanted to lecture them about leaving the local wildlife alone; he wanted to stake them to an anthill and watch them writhe; but, he figured they'd learned their lesson.

Hopefully, the rest would learn from the incident as well. Few things out here are safe to mess with, he thought, and the sooner you learned that the longer you lived.

He felt bad about having to kill the elk until Hightower walked up to him.

"Good shootin', Ben," he said. "That's a lot of good fresh meat for our meals, and you didn't ruin the hide. I can skin him and make a blanket out of that hide."

Ben smiled. Leave it to Hightower, he thought, raised by the Indians to see the practical side of a situation. He'd only had elk meat once before, and remembered that it did taste good; a bit gamier than beef, but in a nice way, and a lot less fat.

"Okay," Ben said. "You need help with it?"

"Yeah, I figure Hezekiah and Journeyman can help me."

He called the two and they walked over to the elk carcass and set to skinning and butchering it.

Three by three, the woodcutters filtered into camp. The old sergeant, still chewing a foul looking lump of tobacco, walked over to Ben.

"Everbody's a mite shook up over what happened today," he said. "I reckon we'se got 'nough timber. So, we kin head back to the fort tomorrow."

"Are you knockin' off for the day?" Ben asked.

"No." The sergeant shook his head. "We'se goin' back out after lunch and trim the last logs and load a few. In the mornin', whatever's left, we loads 'em up, and head on back to the fort."

Which was just as well, Ben thought. Good woodcutters they might be, but he wasn't sure they were cut out to survive in the true wild. He couldn't even imagine what they'd be likely to get up to next, and he worried that it might endanger his men. They couldn't get the logs loaded fast enough for him.

After the mid-day meal was finished, Ben had most of the detachment stay close to the woodcutters as they took the wagons out to where they'd been stacking logs. They were there as much to keep the men from wandering off and getting into more trouble as they were to keep trouble away. Hightower, Layton, and Keller stayed at camp, to guard it primarily, but also to prepare chunks of the elk to roast for the evening meal.

By the time the sun was sinking low in the west, and the aroma of roasting elk meat was hanging in the air around the camp site, the fear of the morning had been relegated to that place in the mind where unpleasant things are stored. Except for the four guards, who stood alert at the four sides of the quadrangle formed by the now almost fully loaded wagons, everyone sat around the cook fire, eating the freshly roasted elk along with beans and corn pone that Hightower and the others had prepared. Faces were greasy and there was much satisfied belching.

"This'll teach that danged deer to mess with me," the man who'd almost been gored said.

"It's an elk, not a deer," Hightower said from the other side of the fire.

"Elk, deer," the man said around a mouthful of meat. "Don't make no difference; still taste good."

The rest of the meal want much the same way, with jokes and jibes traded back and forth across the fire. The woodcutters even seemed to lose some of their nervousness about being around Ben and his men, and Ben noticed that the detachment, even Toussaint, seemed at ease with men they considered only a step above civilians.

Thankfully, when everyone's belly was filled to near bursting, no one felt like singing. That, Ben knew, might be pushing

Toussaint's acceptance of the woodcutters over the limit. Ben posted four sentries, warning them to stay awake and alert, and then went to sit by the now dying cook fire.

He spread out his bedroll near the fire instead of in the tent he shared with Toussaint, preferring to watch the stars as he drifted off to sleep instead of the inside of a tent. The ripsaw sound of snoring from a nearby tent was another reason; he had no desire to be cooped up in a tent with a snoring Toussaint.

Lying there, his head on his saddle and his blanket across his knees, he gazed up at the inky sky, dotted with twinkling stars. He was just drifting into sleep when he heard a hissing sound.

"Psst, Ben," Malachi Davis said from beyond the wagon on the west side of the enclosure. "S-sergeant, you awake?"

Something in the man's voice yanked Ben fully awake. He kicked his blanket aside and sat up.

"Yeah, Malachi," he said quietly. "I'm awake. What's wrong?"

"I ain't sure. Maybe you'd best come and take a look."

Ben walked around the wagon to stand next to the young private.

"What is it, Malachi?"

"Look out yonder. And, listen," Davis said. The fear in his voice was palpable.

Ben looked out into the darkness. At first, he saw only darkness. But, little by little, he began to make out glowing spots about two feet off the ground that seemed to float lazily around. Then, he noticed that the yellow spots seemed to move in pairs, and as he listened, he could hear a snuffling sound, and a low almost subvocal growling. There was an odor in the air, one that seemed to be familiar. As his mind began processing what he was seeing, hearing, and smelling, and the thought of what he was seeing out there in the darkness began to clarify, the hairs on the back of his neck stood on end.

He returned to the cook fire. Picking up a small branch from the firewood near the fire, he lit the end. When it was burning well, he returned to Davis's guard position. The little torch only cast a glow out about four feet, and the glowing lights were ten to fifteen feet away. Ben pulled his arm back and threw the burning branch in the direction of the lights.

As it neared, the lights began to scatter, but not before Ben had gotten a good look.

"Oh, Jesus," Davis said.

"This is not good," Ben said.

11.

The torch struck the ground, sending sparks flying. The large, gray creatures nearest the point of impact scurried away from the dreaded fire.

Before the torch flickered out, Ben counted at least six Mexican Gray Wolves, the infamous *lobo*, staring at the camp site. There were more in the darkness beyond from the sounds. When the flames died, the bright spots that were their eyes reflecting the light of the cook fire came back. Ben tried to calm his breathing and scanned the darkness, counting the pairs of light. The task was made difficult because the wolves continued to skulk back and forth, but he figured there were at least twenty. A couple of the ones he'd seen in the torch light had stood over three feet at the shoulder, with fangs at least nine inches long, razor sharp and deadly looking.

While wolves occasionally raided farms and ranches, pulling down livestock, Ben had never heard of them attacking people. There was, though, a first time for everything, and the smell of the butchered and roasted elk had to be tempting to the carnivores. Ben couldn't be sure that hunger wouldn't cause the wolves to attack the camp, human presence or not.

He decided to take no chances.

"Everybody, wake up," he shouted. "Get your weapons and a torch and come here."

The men assembled. There was general grumbling until a large gray wolf, the largest Ben had ever seen in his life, moved out of the shadows just enough that he could be seen.

"Oh, Lord," one of the woodcutters said. "Wolves. They gone eat us."

"Wolves don't eat people," Ben said. He tried to put conviction in his voice. "They were attracted by the scent of the elk we killed." Then, he had an idea. "If we build a fire around the wagons they won't bother us. They're afraid of fire."

He hoped he was right as the men set about stacking kindling and branches in a large circle around the four wagons. The horses were now reacting to the smell of the wolves, some of whom had come in closer.

When the wood was stacked, Ben took a burning stick from the cook fire and lit it. The fire started slowly, but in a few minutes had encircled them, causing the wolves to retreat a bit. But, they didn't run away.

Everyone in camp was now awake and outside the enclosure, standing behind the ring of fire watching fearfully as the glowing eyes of the wolves continued to circle around them. Ben walked completely around the circle, noting that, while most of the wolves were on the northwest side, a few were sniffing around the other sides as well.

Toussaint, city bred, had never encountered wolves before, especially wolves as large and lethal looking as the Mexican Gray Wolf, and for all his toughness was frightened.

"What we gone do, Ben?" he asked. He kept his voice calm with an effort. His eyes were wide with fright.

Ben felt a clutch of fear in his gut as well, but knew that he had to exert supreme will to keep even a trace from showing.

"We keep the fire going, low, but going," he said. "And, we continue to walk around the perimeter so they can see us. Wolves usually attack weak animals in a herd, and

I've never heard of them attacking a man."

Toussaint looked skeptical at first, but as time passed and the wolves came no closer to the fire, he relaxed. Seeing Ben and Toussaint calm eased the fears of the others.

No one wanted to go back to sleep, but Ben knew they would need to be rested, so he assigned four men to do sentry duty in two-hour shifts, while the rest tried to sleep, although for most of them sleep wouldn't come.

And, it went like that until the sky showed the first colors of the coming dawn. By the time there was enough light to see, the wolves had decided that the fire and the two-legged upright creatures were two hard a target and had melted into the forest. Breakfast was eaten with much glancing over shoulders and Ben left four guards on the site while the others accompanied the woodcutters out to load the remaining cut timber.

By noon, the timber was loaded and the camp site was struck. The men opted for eating jerky on the trail rather than cooking over the fire. They washed the jerky down with water from their canteens. They didn't stop looking nervously over their shoulders until they were almost in sight of Fort Union.

12.

Ben and his detachment were given another day of rest after their return with the timber. Most of it was spent cleaning and replacing equipment.

On the second day after their return, Major Wainwright summoned Ben to his office right after breakfast.

"Sergeant Carter," the major said after Ben had seated himself in front of his desk. "I have an assignment for you and your men that I think will be a welcome change."

Ben looked skeptical, but the officer acted as if he didn't see the look on his face.

"We recently purchased cattle from a Texas rancher," Wainwright continued. "And, he's driven them to Clayton over on the border. He refuses to drive them all the way here to the fort unless we pay almost double the asking price. So, I'm sending you and your crew to Clayton to bring them home."

Ben's mouth dropped open.

"Sir, I've never driven cattle before. I was raised on a farm."

"Yes, I know that," Wainwright said dismissively. "But, you have at least two men who grew up around cattle. Besides, how hard could it be to drive a few hundred dumb cows from Clayton to here?"

How hard indeed, Ben thought. I can't even answer the question, because I have no idea. He knew, though, that the decision had been made. He stood and saluted.

"Yes, sir," he said. "We'll do our best. When do you want us to leave for Clayton?"

"Well, it's 130 miles to Clayton. Getting there will take you about three days. Probably take you four or five days coming back. So, I'd say you should leave immediately."

Immediately was three hours later. After informing the detachment of their new mission, Ben had to get extra pack horses, rations for ten days to be safe, and check all their gear and equipment. After talking to Buckley, who had been on several cattle drives before joining the cavalry, he decided that the only gear they would ride with would be their bedroll, carbine, pistol, and saber. The rest of their gear would be distributed among five pack animals; one animal for each two troopers. When he was satisfied that all was in order, the detachment struck out, heading northeast toward the great rolling plains that stretched to the border with Texas and Oklahoma to the east and Colorado to the north.

By the end of the first day, they made it to just south of Springer, an unremarkable town of mostly adobe structures sitting on the plains that rolled away from the Sangre de Cristo Mountains. Ben had the men make camp in a clearing surrounded by medium height pine trees. He figured that since they would have to camp out once they picked up the cattle in Clayton, they might as well get used to it.

Ben paid particular attention to the terrain as they rode, noting the rivers and streams they would have to cross coming back, and where the best pastures for night grazing were, and mentally planning the best route for the drive. Between Fort Union and Springer, the only water course of any significance was the Mora River, which ran shallow and sluggish from the lack of rain. Its broad, flat banks would pose no problem.

The next day, after they ate and struck camp, they rode quickly through Springer, taking the trail east toward Clayton. Just east of the town, they encountered the Canadian River. Like the Mora, it wasn't deep, but the current was swift in places. Ben sent the detachment on ahead and, along with Hightower, scouted north and south along the river to find a good place to drive a herd across. Hightower found a broad expanse north of the trail, where the current was relatively slow. The sand banks would slow them down, but they wouldn't risk losing cattle to the rushing water.

They made it halfway to Clayton on the second day, camping on the banks of Ute Creek for the night.

At noon on the third day, they arrived in Clayton.

The first stop in New Mexico Territory on the Santa Fe Trail, Clayton was little more than a settlement straddling the ruts of the many wagon trains that had traversed the region enroute to Santa Fe. A collection of adobe huts, interspersed with a few *residencias* of the wealthier establishments, the main street, running northeast to southwest paralleling the Santa Fe Trail, was dominated by saloons and stores selling ranching supplies and goods for use on the cattle drives which, along with it being a stopover on the trail, was the settlement's main source of income. Texas cattle ranchers from the Panhandle and the plains of West Texas driving their cattle to the markets in Atchison, Kansas, used Clayton as a stopover.

The population, mostly Mexican, but with an increasing number of whites, was about one thousand permanent residents, but during the season when cattle were being driven to market, it often reached three thousand.

It sat in the shadow of Rabbit Ear Mountain, the first two peaks of the Rocky Mountains. The mountains looked nothing like rabbit ears; they had served as a lookout for Cheyenne Indians who had lived in the area since before the arrival of the Spanish. When wagon trains began invading their hunting grounds, the Indians, who could follow the progress of the slow moving caravans from the peaks, would attack them. The Spanish governor sent cavalry to attack the Cheyenne village. During the attack, the chief, *Orejas de Conejos*, or Rabbit Ears, was killed. The mountains were later named for him.

The eastern side of the settlement, looking over a shallow valley covered with knee-high grass and merging into a thick forest, was where the transiting herds were kept. It was here that Ben found the rancher who had sold the cattle to the army.

A barrel-chested man with a thick mat of chest hair that protruded from the open neck of his shirt, wiry brown hair, flecked with gray on his bullet-shaped head, covered in dust from the trail, stood at the gate of the hastily erected corral in which the herd of cattle grazed. Five cowboys stood off to the side watching the soldiers approach.

"Y'all the soldiers from up Fort Union?" he asked as Ben swung out of the saddle.

"That's correct," Ben said. "You're the owner?"

The man's eyes narrowed. He rubbed the stubble on his chin.

"Yeah, that be me," he said finally. "Sam Putnam."

"Sergeant Ben Carter, Ninth Cavalry," Ben said formally. "I assume you have the bill of sale?"

"You boys know anything 'bout drivin' cattle?"

The cowboys snickered, and Ben heard one mutter, "Probly know 'bout bein' drove *like* cattle." He kept his face impassive, as still as if it had been carved from dark wood, his gaze locked with the elderly rancher.

"Enough to get them from here to Fort Union," he said, his voice even and emotionless.

Looking past Ben, the rancher Putnam could see that the expressions on the faces of the men in his detachment were just as stony, and they all rested their hands lightly on the carbines attached to their saddles. He didn't know what they knew about cattle drives, but he'd heard stories about their exploits in battle.

"Well," he said. "No skin offen my nose." He pulled a folded paper from his shirt pocket and passed it to Ben. "This here's the bill o' sale, all proper signed and notarized. It transfers 150 head of prime beef to Fort Union, to be picked up here in Clayton by troopers from the fort. I reckon that'd be you boys. Good luck gettin' 'em the rest of the way. We done drove 'em 110 miles already, from my ranch over near Amarillo, and iffen you ain't got no questions, I'd like to be headin' back that way. This town's 'bout as dull as watchin' grass grow, and they water the whisky."

Ben took the paper and read it carefully, satisfying himself that it said what the man claimed. Done reading, he folded it and tucked it inside his tunic. He glanced at the milling cattle. He wasn't about to waste time counting each animal, assuming the rancher would be hesitant to try and short the army.

"Everything seems to be in order," he said. "Thank you very much. We'll take over from here."

Without waiting for the man's acknowledgement, Ben turned to face his men.

"Sergeant Toussaint, take charge of setting up camp. Corporals Hightower and Buckley, come with me to check the herd."

The rancher and his cowboys stood mouths agape for a few minutes, watching the soldiers quickly set up tents and a cook fire, and construct a makeshift corral from branches, pieces of wood and brush for the horses. With Hightower and Buckley flanking him, Ben pulled aside the gate of the fence that the cowboys had constructed of the same material, and rode through.

"Well, Charles," Ben said when they were out of earshot of the gawking Texans, who were now moving toward their horses anyway. "This look like 150 cows to you?"

Buckley stood up in his stirrups, scanning in a full circle.

"Close enough not to matter," he said. "We're likely to lose one or two that stray off 'tween here and the fort anyway."

Ben's eyebrows lifted.

"Is it usual to lose cows when you drive them?" he asked.

Buckley laughed.

"You ain't never done nothin' like this before, have you?" Ben shook his head. "That's what I thought. Well, the answer is, yeah, one or two likely to stray off at night and not be missed. Wolves might pull down a couple if they fall behind. And, you call 'em cattle, not cows. Some of 'em just happen to be bulls, and some of 'em are steers."

"Isn't a bull a cow? And, what in blazes is a steer?"

Buckley laughed again, so hard he almost fell from his saddle. Hightower joined him.

"Ben," Hightower said. "As long as a bull's got all his equipment, he ain't nowhere near bein' a cow. A cow is a female, and a bull is female. When you remove a bull's man parts he's called a steer."

Ben shook his head.

"I sort of get it. We had cows back home. My pa showed me how to milk them. And, we had an old bull. I never saw a steer, though. And, I don't think I even want to know how they get that way.

Buckley had recovered from his laughing fit, and he gazed at Ben over his horse's neck.

"This," he said to Hightower. "Is goin' to be one long cattle drive."

Charles Ray

13.

Ben roused everyone the next morning before the sun rose. He had them prepare breakfast in the dark, and strike the camp as soon as they finished eating. He wanted to get the cattle moving toward the fort as soon as it was light enough to see.

While the men were saddling their horses, Ben pulled Buckley aside.

"Okay, Charles," he said. "Here's how it's going to be. You're in charge of the cattle drive. If we're attacked, I'll take command. Otherwise, everyone, me included follow your orders."

Buckley puffed out his chest.

"Finally, I git to be a trail boss," he said. "When I worked on the ranch, whenever we'd go on a drive, I was always the wrangler."

"What's a wrangler?" Ben asked.

"That's the one that handles the *remuda*, the extra horses," Buckley said. "That job usually goes to the youngest cowboy on the drive, but bein' the only black man on my boss's ranch, it always went to me. I reckon that'd be good duty for Malachi, him bein' the youngest in the detachment and all."

"Okay, what else?"

"Well, since you might have to take over if we get hit by cattle thieves you ought to ride up front with me; that's where the trail boss rides. That leaves seven. I'm thinkin' we have three on each flank to keep the critters from strayin', and one ridin' drag to keep the back end of the herd movin'."

"Okay, I'll tell the others you're in charge, and you assign duties," Ben said.

"One other thing, Ben; once everybody gets the hang of it, we might be able to make near 20, 25 miles a day, but at first we need to take it slow. I reckon today, if we do 15 miles that'll be enough. We need to stop and let 'em graze before it gets dark, and there ought to be at least two night guards, so we don't want to overtire the fellas."

"I'm thinking you and me should do the first shift tonight," Ben said.

"I was kind of thinkin' you'd say that,"

Buckley said.

Ben gathered the detachment, and told them that Buckley would be in charge of the drive, which didn't surprise any of them. Buckley then outlined everyone's duties. He assigned Holman to the drag position first, eliciting a loud groan from the lanky corporal.

"I ain't never been on no cattle drive," Holman said. "But, even I know that the one ridin' behind the herd gets to eat all the dust them critters stir up."

"That's why you have to make sure you keep your scarf over your face all the time," Buckley said. "I'll spell the drag every two hours, so every one of you gone get your chance to eat dust."

"Me too?" asked young Malachi Davis who hadn't been thrilled at being made the wrangler.

"Yeah, Malachi, even you," Buckley said. "Now, we gone take it slow and easy the first two days. I figure we try and do 'bout 15 miles. I'll try and find a good spot for night grazin', and we can pitch camp before dark."

"I can scout for grazing land," Ben said. "That way, you can keep your eye on the herd all the time."

Buckley nodded. He then had everyone line up in their assigned locations, and kicked open the makeshift gate. He'd had his eye on a large, gray Brahma bull who seemed a natural herd leader. He rode alongside the animal and poked at it with his boot, moving it toward the open gate. After a few minutes, the old bull shook his head and began to move slowly toward the gate. As Buckley figured, the rest of the herd docilely followed.

It was only a matter of minutes for 150 animals to clear the enclosure, and it was accomplished without incident. He angled the old bull a bit south and then west to go around rather than through Clayton.

Riding alongside him, Ben was impressed with how smoothly Buckley handled the situation. He might have been only a wrangler on drives before, but he'd been observant and had learned well. Things were getting off to a good start. Ben hadn't known what to expect, so everything was something of a surprise to him. He'd thought, for instance, that when the drive started, the animals would be strung out in a long, ragged line. Instead, they grouped themselves in a wedge formation with the old bull at the apex, followed by the stronger animals, and with the weaker bringing up the rear.

"When we get to that first creek," Buckley said to Ben. "I'm gone need you to help me keep that old bull movin' straight."

"That shouldn't be a problem," Ben said.

"You never know. Cattle is 'bout the dumbest critters on earth. That old bull could get distracted by a floatin' leaf and turn around, and the rest would follow him. They'd start millin' 'round in that creek and some of the weaker ones could drown. Ain't to safe if a man on a horse get himself caught up in it either. When I worked on the ranch, we'd lose a man to drownin' just 'bout ever drive."

At that sobering bit of news, some of Ben's earlier euphoria evaporated.

Ben learned just how serious Buckley was at the first stream they encountered, Carrizo Creek, a few miles west of Clayton. A north-south flowing creek, twenty yards wide at the ford, it didn't look deep, but the current was brisk. At first, the lead bull simply headed straight across, but as he neared midstream where the water came up to his muzzle he paused and began looking right and left. The trailing animals stopped and began shuffling against each other and making mournful sounds.

"Ben, move in close and keep his head pointed toward the other bank," Buckley yelled from the right side of the bull. "If he starts turnin', we likely to lose control of the rest."

The riders on the flanks, their horses up to their bellies in the cool water, were yelling at the confused bovines, trying to keep them from wandering off. Journeyman Keller, who had spelled Holman riding drag, watched from the east bank, happy that he was no longer being assaulted by the dust kicked up by the herd, but worried about his companions who were dangerously close to the confused animals.

Ben rode in close to the bull, yelling and trying to coax it to continue its forward movement. The animal stopped dead in its tracks, looking from side to side, wild-eyed confusion in its eyes and a deep rumbling sound coming from its throat. Ben was close enough now on the left side for his horse's flanks to occasionally brush the bull's side, and Buckley had moved in just as close on the right. He added his voice to Ben's in an effort to get the beast moving again.

"What's the matter with him?" Ben asked. "Why won't he start moving?"

"Who knows?" Buckley replied with a note of exasperation in his voice. "These critters is the dumbest animals ever put on this earth. Just keep yellin' at him, it'll get to his brain pretty soon." He leaned over and smacked the animal's neck with his fist. "Move on, you big tub of lard. You ain't got but one way to go."

The bull swung its head in Buckley's direction, and made an almost high-pitched sound, and then, as if it understood his words, turned back toward the far bank and plunged forward. The rest of the herd slowly coalesced and followed.

By the time the herd and everyone, including Davis and the pack animals, were on the opposite bank, Ben was drenched, partly in water from the creek, partly in sweat, and breathing as if he'd just run a mile.

"Is it gonna be that way every time we have to cross water?" he asked Buckley.

The Texan shrugged.

"Ain't no way of knowin'," he said. He looked up. The sun was nearly at its zenith. "Hell fire, we might's well stop here for food and rest."

A broad field of grass stretched westward from the stream, and the cattle began grazing immediately. They took turns, two at a time, guarding the herd to prevent strays, while the rest ate a lunch of bacon, beans, biscuits, and coffee around a hastily built cook fire.

They rested, men and horses, for twenty minutes, and then formed up and started the herd moving west again.

Ben rode ahead to scout for streams and

the best crossing places, and to look for a place to stop for the night. As he rode, he thought that he'd found an occupation that made being a soldier look good. Driving cattle was a dirty, smelly, dangerous occupation. If the 150 animals they were shepherding back to the fort was anything to go by, cowboys who drove as many as 3,000 animals from Texas to Abilene, Kansas, a journey that often took up to a month, had it worse than any soldier. It was no wonder, he thought, that they often went plumb wild when they hit one of the many cow towns that dotted the trails north, or when they finally arrived at the railhead and the end of a drive. After days of eating dust and smelling cows, of fearing getting caught in a stampede or being knocked off your horse in the middle of s river as the dumb beasts milled around in confusion, blowing off steam with watered down whisky and heavily painted ladies of the evening was understandable.

14.

While the drive didn't get any less dirty, and the smell seemed to have worked its way into the fabric of their uniforms, the men were quick learners, and managed to increase from 15 miles a day the first two days, to near 20 miles a day, coming within 15 miles of the town of Springer by the end of the fourth day on the trail.

They cut southeast of the town and then turned the herd toward the southwest for the last leg, a fifty-mile stretch that fortunately was carpeted with grass, giving them many places to graze the herd at rest stops.

On the evening of the sixth day, they were just north of the Mora River, no more than a day or two from the end of their journey. They'd found a broad plain covered in sweet grass, and cut by a small stream that flowed into the Mora. By the time the sun was a half-disk on the horizon, they'd put out two men to keep the herd from straying, built a cook fire, constructed a makeshift corral for the horses, and got the evening meal going.

Corporal Lucas Hall had the cook duty that day, and after he'd washed the dust of the trail from his face, hair, and body and started the meal, the others went to the stream, upstream from the herd, to wash. Their dark blue tunics were a dusty yellow from six days of dust, and no matter how they beat them against the small tree trunks or over rocks, the dust wouldn't come out. Even after disrobing and washing, they could feel the gritty dust in their mouths, eyes, hair and ears.

"I'm gone be tastin' dust for the next six months," complained Nat Tatum.

"It's like it done got inside my skin," Marcus Scott added.

"Just one more day, and we can scrub it off," Ben said, although he too felt as if he'd been covered in dust and grime forever. He could feel the grit when he blinked. "I think we're gonna have to get new uniforms, though."

"That the only thing good to come out of this," Journeyman Keller said. "These uniforms so old they startin' to fall apart anyway."

Everyone, Ben included, laughed.

Buckley sent Keller and Scott out to replace the two guards, Hightower and Layton, to allow them to wash.

As they sat around the cook fire eating, some of their good spirit returned, despite being sore and bone weary from so many hours in the saddle.

Hezekiah Layton had replaced Malachi Davis as wrangler for the day, and Davis had been riding drag for the last two hours before they stopped.

"You know," he said as he sopped up his beans with a corn pone. "I never knowed cows could smell so bad."

"They smell like animals," Toussaint said.

"Naw," Davis said, shaking his head. "It ain't just the animal smell. It like gas. I rode too close one time, and it made my eyes water."

"That'll teach you not to ride to close to the hind end of a cow," Buckley said, laughing. "You done breathed in a whole bunch of cow farts. You think it's bad with this many, you try ridin' behind a herd of over a thousand. Them critters eat the grass at one end and pass it out the rear, and a good part of it is gas so strong you don't want to light a fire close to it."

Davis made a face.

"Ben, if it all right with you, I don't mind goin' back to bein' wrangler for the rest of the trip," he said.

"Aw, I don't mind bein' wrangler," Layton said.

Davis looked as if he'd cry.

"Let me sleep on it," Ben said, leaving both men looking befuddled.

While everyone enjoyed sitting around the fire poking fun at Layton and Davis, Buckley reminded them that the guards had to change every two hours, and they needed to get back on the trail at first light, so they drifted off to their bedrolls, having foregone erecting tents.

Ben had the midnight watch with Buckley, and was pulling his blanket aside when the Texan leaned over him. In the dim light from the dying embers of the cook fire, Ben saw that Buckley had a finger to his lips.

"What's the matter?" Ben whispered.

"Somethin's wrong with the herd," Buckley whispered back. "Listen."

At first, Ben heard nothing. But, as he

listened, he noticed what had spooked Buckley. He'd drifted off to sleep to the low shuffling sound a densely packed herd of cattle makes, but there was a disruption in that sound now, little low grumbles and snorts as if some of the animals were being spooked by something.

"What do you think it is?" Ben asked.

"Somethin's got inside the herd."

Quietly, the two men walked to the corral and retrieved their horses, and just as quietly, saddled them. When they'd mounted, both drew their carbines from the saddle mounts. They gently urged the animals toward the milling herd.

Buckley leaned over toward Ben. "I'll work 'round to the left, and you take the right. The guards are over to the other side, and we need to work quietly 'round to 'em."

Ben nodded and started his horse walking around the right side of the herd. In the darkness, he could just make out the bodies of the nearest animals. The far side of the herd was cloaked in darkness.

When he was about halfway around the mass of animals, ahead of him, two dark shapes detached themselves from the larger body. The shapes were at first indistinct, but as Ben drew nearer, he saw that it was a smallish person, followed by one of the herd animals. He kicked his horse into a gallop.

The figure stopped at the sound of Ben's horse, and then, dashed away. But, it was too late. Ben was already almost upon him. He debated shooting, but something held him back. Instead, he rode up alongside the fleeing figure and swung at its head with the butt of his carbine, sending it sprawling face down.

Ben swung out of the saddle and ran back to the figure, calling for the others as he ran.

"Charles, fellas," he yelled. "It was a cow thief spooking the herd. I got him over here."

George Toussaint, awakened by Ben's yelling, grabbed a burning stick from the cook fire and blew on it to cause it to flame up, and using it as a torch, ran out to where Ben stood over the prone figure.

In the flickering light of the torch, they saw that it was an Indian, small of stature. Ben knelt and rolled the body over.

"Did you kill him?" Toussaint asked.

Ben looked down and saw that the thief was little more than a boy, probably in his mid-teens. He felt for a pulse behind the boy's jaw, and was rewarded with an erratic, but strong beat.

"No, he's alive," he said. "But, I conked him on the head pretty hard. Help me get him back to camp."

With Toussaint's help, Ben lifted the boy, who seemed to weigh little, and carried him back to the camp. They lay him on the ground. Ben examined his head, while Toussaint stoked up the fire to give more light. By now, everyone was awake, and except for Buckley, and Holman who had taken Ben's turn for the midnight watch, the entire detachment was gathered around the supine figure.

In the light, he looked even younger. Dressed in dusty buckskin pants and a tattered shirt over which he wore a leather vest, he looked like a child. And, an undernourished child at that, Ben thought. His face was gaunt, and as Ben felt his chest area to check his breathing, he could feel his ribs. They seemed awfully close to the surface of his skin.

The boy's eyelids flickered twice, and then he opened his eyes. It took him some seconds to focus, and when he did to see several dark faces looking down at him, his eyes widened in terror. He scrambled to sit up, but Ben applied gentle pressure on his chest to hold him down. Silently, he thrashed and pushed against the pressure.

"He ain't nothin' but a kid," Toussaint said. "And, he look scared to death."

"From his condition, he looks hungry too," Ben said. "I wish he could understand me so I could make him understand we don't plan to hurt him."

The boy stopped thrashing and gazed up at Ben. The two held each other's gaze. After a long moment, the boy's body relaxed and the look of terror left his eyes.

"I understand the white man's talk," he said quietly and hoarsely.

Ben's eyes widened in surprise.

"You speak English? Where'd you learn it?"

"When the soldiers moved my tribe to the reservation, a white man came to teach us. My father sent me to the school to learn the ways of the whites."

"What's your name, and why were you trying to steal our cattle?" Ben asked.

"I am Little Elk. My father is chief of the Elk Clan of the Jicarilla Apache. We of the Elk Clan are Ollero Jicarilla, and want peace with the whites. They moved us to land where there is no game to hunt, but promised that we would be provided food.

Little Elk's expression saddened.

"But, the white man lied. Sometimes many moons go by and no food is given to us. When it comes, it is rotten. Our young ones cry at night from hunger. Many have died, and yet the white man does nothing. As eldest son of the chief, I have led other young braves from the reservation to find food so that more do not die."

"There are others out there?" Ben asked.

Little Elk regarded Ben with suspicion. But, something in Ben's expression must have convinced him that this dark soldier could be trusted.

"Yes, three other braves wait beyond the stream. If I had been able to get away with the animal, another would have tried."

"Do you have horses? How were you planning to get stolen cattle back to your people?"

"We have six horses. We would have killed the cows and carried the meat and hides on the two extra horses. What will you do with me now?"

Ben hadn't given any thought to that. On the one hand, the boy had been caught red handed stealing, and could be taken back to Fort Union for trial. On the other, he *was* just a boy, and he was being starved. Ben looked around at the other soldiers.

"What do you reckon we should do with him, George?" he asked Toussaint, who was his second in command.

"I know what it like to be hungry," Toussaint said. "And, 'sides, if we take him back to the fort, it mean somebody got to keep watch on him. And, somebody gone have to keep watch for his friends, 'case they decide to try and get him back. We need everybody to keep these dumb critters movin'. Hell, I say just let him go. We got the cow back, so no real harm done."

There were murmurs around the group, and nods of agreement. White Elk looked from one face to another, a look of disbelief on his broad, bronzed face.

"But," Ben said. "They're still starving. If I let him go, he'll just try and steal beef somewhere else. If he gets caught by one of the ranchers around here, or one of the cowboys from Texas, they'll likely just hang him or shoot him."

"Hm, hadn't thought of that," Toussaint said. "What you think we ought to do?"

"Well, Charles said sometimes on drives, cattle stray off and get lost," he said. "What if four got lost from this herd?"

"You sayin' what I think you sayin',"

Toussaint asked.

Ben nodded. "It would sort of solve two problems."

Ben looked down at Little Elk.

"If we give you four steers, will you promise to go back to your reservation?"

"You would do that?" There was a look of complete disbelief on the young Indian's face.

"I would," Ben said. "Only if you promise to go back to the reservation and stop trying to steal cattle."

"You would accept my promise?"

Ben nodded. Little Elk raised his right hand and laid it on Ben's right shoulder.

"You have my promise," he said.

15.

The rest of the drive was without incident. Buckley pushed a bit harder the next day, and they drove the herd into the corral at Fort Union just before the sun set.

They then made a beeline for the bathhouse, and spent an hour scrubbing the dust and grime from their bodies. Scrubbed and in a fresh uniform, Ben reported to Major Wainwright to hand over the bill of sale. He then went to the mess, ate a light supper, and returned to the barracks, where the rest of the detachment had already crawled into their bunks and were sleeping their first restful sleep in over a week. It didn't take Ben long to join them.

The next morning, after mess, Ben was summoned to Wainwright's office. The major had a frown on his face when Ben entered.

"Have a seat, sergeant," he said, lazily returning Ben's salute. "I had the quartermaster sergeant check the herd you brought in. Seems to be four head missing. You lose any strays?"

Ben could have agreed, knowing the rest of the detachment would back him up, but he'd always been taught to tell the truth no matter how unpleasant the consequences.

"No, sir," he said. He then told Wainwright of their encounter with Little Elk and his companions.

When Ben had finished, Wainwright's expression had softened, but he still frowned.

"You're to be commended for your compassion, sergeant," he said. "But, those animals were army property, and you had no authority to do what you did. You could be court martialed for it, but I'm not doing that to a soldier with your record. Instead, you'll have to pay for the four animals out of your pay. For four head, it'll come to a hundred dollars. Do you have that much cash?"

Unlike many of the troopers, Ben didn't spend his month's pay within the first week after receiving it in the tent city outside the fort, he didn't drink, and he didn't gamble. The adjutant offered storage in his safe for the rare few who, like Ben, saved some of their pay. Despite his frugality, though, Ben probably had fifty dollars saved. If the remaining amount was taken out of his pay, which as a line sergeant amounted to twenty-three dollars per month, he would be dead broke for the next two months; no pay and no savings.

"I got enough to pay half of it," he said.

Wainwright was not without sympathy. He decided to dock half Ben's pay for the balance, which would leave him with just over eleven dollars a month for four months. It would hurt, but it was better than being broke.

Back in the barracks, Ben sat on the end of his bunk and thought about the outcome of this period of 'easy duty,' and wished he'd been left in the field. The men of the detachment had been there when he returned, and when he told them what had happened with the major, they left him alone. Which was just as well for him, he thought; he wasn't exactly pleasant company at that moment.

Ben was not one to sulk for long, though. He'd made a decision and was prepared to accept the consequences of that decision.

He was polishing his boots when George Toussaint came running into the barracks.

"Ben, you got to come outside," Toussaint said breathlessly.

"Why?" Ben asked.

"Just come on and look."

Reluctantly, Ben rose and followed Toussaint to the door of the barracks. As he emerged from the building, he saw a line of troopers heading toward the commander's office. As men in the line saw him, some waved.

"What's going on?" Ben asked.

Toussaint placed a large dark hand on Ben's shoulder.

"Well, Ben; when the other fellas heard you was gone have to pay for them four missin' steers, they all sort of decided to chip in to pay for you."

Speechless, Ben walked along the line of men, nodding at those who greeted him or patted his shoulder as he passed. He found a bemused Wainwright standing in front of the headquarters building.

Ben came to a halt in front of the major, and saluted. Wainwright wearily returned the salute.

"Uh, Sergeant Carter," he said. "Could I talk to you privately?

Ben nodded and followed Wainwright inside. Wainwright motioned him to the chair in front of his desk.

"Looks like we have ourselves a problem, sergeant," Wainwright said after he'd seated himself behind the desk. "Seems the rest of the men in the unit think I'm wrong to make you pay for the missing cattle. Matter of fact, a few of the officers feel the same way."

"Sir, I had nothing to do with this," Ben said. "I can talk to them if you want me to."

Wainwright waved dismissively.

"No, sergeant, there's no need for that. I'm not blaming you. Hell, you didn't have to tell me what you did, and I admire your honesty. The men are saying that if I insist on payment for the animals, they'll chip in from their pay to do it. Not many soldiers can inspire that kind of loyalty, sergeant. I'm impressed."

So, in fact, was Ben. He had no idea that the rank and file of the troop even knew more than his name. He never socialized with them on those rare occasions when he was in the fort; nor did he drink and gamble with his fellow sergeants.

"I can't let them do that, sir," he said. "It's my responsibility, and I'll take care of it myself. I'll go out and tell them."

"No, you won't," Wainwright said, holding up a hand. "This is a problem that is my responsibility as commander to solve, and it seems to me the best solution all around would be to just write off the animals. Losing four strays actually isn't all that bad, considering you and your men had no experience in driving cattle. I haven't done my report to regiment yet anyway."

"Major, I'm not comfortable with you having to file a false report to protect me."

"Better that than having to report to regiment that I have a mutiny on my hands, sergeant."

Ben knew the pressure the man faced; in many ways far greater than any he'd faced being the man in charge in the field. And, just as he'd had to do in the field, this was a situation Wainwright would have to deal with alone.

"I reckon you know better than me, sir," he said. "I appreciate what you're doing."

Wainwright seemed to be staring off into the far distance. At first, Ben thought he might not even have heard what he'd just said. Then, the officer blinked.

"Not necessary, sergeant," he said. "I'm doing this for the whole unit. Now, you go on back to your barracks. I have another job for you tomorrow, and you'll need to be rested for it. I'll take care of the men."

Ben stood and saluted. He followed

Wainwright back outside where the whole unit had gathered, including several of the lieutenants and captains; a sea of dark and white faces. Wainwright patted Ben on the shoulder and gently pushed him toward the barracks, and then turned to face the milling, murmuring crowd.

The cheer that followed his brief announcement was music to Ben's ears.

Charles Ray

16.

The next morning, after the 6:00 reveille and assembly, Wainwright pulled Ben aside as the rest of the troop responded to stable call.

"Sergeant," he said. "I have another job for you and your men."

Something in the tone of his voice alerted Ben that the 'job' would be anything but routine.

"I hope it won't have to do with herding any more cattle," Ben said.

"No, no more cattle drives." Wainwright laughed, but his face quickly resumed a serious expression. "This is far more important, and probably even more dangerous."

Ben could seriously think of nothing he could be asked to do that would rival a cattle drive for danger and dirtiness, until

Wainwright told him what he wanted him to do.

"A shipment of gold bullion intended for the army down in El Paso is being shipped from San Francisco to Santa Fe," Wainwright said. "We've been ordered to pick it up in Santa Fe and hold it here until someone from El Paso can come and get it."

Gold bullion, thought Ben. Word of a shipment of gold gets out, and every outlaw west of the Mississippi would be after it, which wouldn't be healthy for anyone escorting it.

"I don't suppose it'd do any good my asking how much, and why we have to do it, would there?" he asked.

"The amount doesn't matter, but just so you know, it's two million dollars' worth. As to why, the army didn't say, just said I was to send a detail to pick it up and deliver it here to be held until someone from Texas comes to get it."

No surprise there. Seldom did the army think its people need to know why they were doing what they were ordered to do. They just wanted it done.

"When do we have to pick it up?"

"It arrives in Santa Fe in five days," Wainwright said. "It might not be a bad idea if you and your men were there before it arrived."

Five days. With the three-day ride to the territorial capital, that only gave Ben a day to prepare.

"Okay, major," he said. "I'll need a few things, though, if I'm going to be able to get that gold back here."

"Anything you need, sergeant; within reason that is."

Wainwright was as good as his word. After Ben had alerted his men, he then scurried around the fort, from stable to armory to quartermaster, and finally to the paymaster. At each, his requests were met with frowns, but when he dropped Wainwright's name, or threatened to call him, they were fulfilled.

From the stable, he got two wagons, each with a team of four horses, and four extra mounts with saddles. At the armory, he drew four carbines, four revolvers, and 150 rounds for each. His request for two Gatling machine guns with 1,000 rounds for each met with some resistance at first, but again, Wainwright's name pried them loose. The quartermaster merely raised his eyebrows when Ben requested four uniforms; especially when he said they didn't have to be new.

Wainwright accompanied him to the

paymaster's office. The paymaster, a junior lieutenant, hesitated when Wainwright directed him to give Ben a thousand dollars in cash.

"What do you need this much money for, sergeant?" the lieutenant asked.

"Renting a wagon and team, and paying men to drive it," Ben said after Wainwright nodded.

"But, aren't you taking wagons and men from the fort?"

"Lieutenant," Wainwright said. "You only need to know so much. Just give the sergeant the money. I'll be personally responsible for it." He looked at Ben. "If he loses any of it, I'm taking it out of his pay."

Ben knew that Wainwright wasn't joking. But, he had what he needed. The next morning, the detachment set out for Santa Fe. Davis and Layton were assigned to drive the two wagons, their horses in the *remuda* under Private First Class Nat Tatum's control.

He pushed hard, stopping only to let the animals rest and get water now and then. It took them two days of hard riding, and they were bone weary and dusty when they pulled into Santa Fe. Rather than checking into a hotel, or putting the wagons or animals in a livery stable, as he'd done on his first visit, he arranged to pitch tents at Fort Marcy, the Ninth's regimental headquarters, located in the capital. With no troops assigned, there wasn't a lot of space at the fort, and more than one staff officer raised an eyebrow at the jumble of tents, men, animals, and wagons tucked into a corner of the fort. The regimental commander, however, had given his personal approval, so nothing was said.

The morning after their arrival, Ben rode into the southern part of the city, where most of the black residents lived.

17.

He walked into a seedy saloon located on a back street. Except for a couple of swarthy Hispanics seated at a table near the door, everyone in the place was black. But, Ben, wearing his uniform, drew attention. Hostile eyes followed him as he walked to the bar. A heavyset man with skin so black it shone with blue highlights from the lanterns over the bar was wiping at the surface of the bar with a grimy rag.

"What you want?" he asked when Ben stepped up to the bar.

"I'm looking for a place where I can buy or rent a wagon and team of horses, and hire six able-bodied men," Ben replied.

The man regarded Ben through narrowed eyes.

"You soldiers ain't got yo own horses? I ain't never seen no black man recruitin' for the army in this part of town befo. In fact, I ain't never seen nobody recruitin' down here in the bottom."

"Well, friend, there's a first time for everything. I need people for a special job. Now, can you point me in the right direction or not?"

"Depends, soldier boy, on what you payin'."

"I'm prepared to discuss that with the person I rent from. As for hiring, you're a bit too old for what I need."

The bartender laughed.

"I wasn't talkin' 'bout hirin' out to you, boy," he said. "But, I jest might be the man you need to talk to 'bout that horse and wagon. Matter of fact, I might jest be able to point you to men you can hire; if the money's right."

Somehow, that didn't surprise Ben. The man was probably the owner of the saloon, working the day shift and keeping an eye on the till. As a businessman, he was probably one of the wealthiest, if not the wealthiest, people in the community. If there was a deal to be made, he was likely the one to make it with.

"How much would a wagon and team of four horses cost me to rent?"

"How long you want 'em for?"

Ben did some quick mental calculations.

"About a week, ten days tops."

"You need a driver, too?"

"No," Ben said. "I'll supply my own driver."

"I can let you have one for two hundred dollars."

The price was outrageous, but Ben needed an extra wagon if the plan he had in mind was to work. On the other hand, if he agreed to quickly, the man might get suspicious.

"I'll give you one fifty," he said.

The bartender smiled, and nodded his head.

"One seventy five," he said. "And, that's my final offer."

"Done," Ben said, and they shook on it. "Now, about hiring those six men."

18.

The bartender took Ben into a back room of the saloon, and had him wait while he sent for men of the community.

They paraded in one at a time, and after interviewing nearly twenty, Ben selected six. They ranged in age from nineteen to thirty; mostly day laborers who were currently unemployed, and for whom the fifty dollars Ben offered for a week's work seemed like a windfall.

He gave them explicit instructions. They were to wait until dark, and meet him near Fort Marcy, and they were to tell no one where they were going.

Ben figured they'd at a minimum tell their friends and family they'd been hired by the black soldier, but beyond telling them to meet him at Fort Marcy, they knew nothing. The success of his plan depended on that.

As promised, after dark, when the area near the fort where Ben had arranged to meet them was cloaked in shadow, the men arrived; first two, then one, then the final three. Ben led them to the area where the detachment had set up camp and had them get inside tents, three to a tent. It was crowded, but it was the best he could do. They were instructed to stay in the tents except to use the slit trench latrine the detachment had dug near a large tree, and then only under the watchful eye of one of the soldiers. Ben assured them they wouldn't be harmed, and that he would explain what he wanted them to do soon. They ate what the soldiers ate, and without complaint.

Near mid-day, Ben went to the rail depot, taking the two wagons and half the detachment, leaving the rest at Fort Marcy under Toussaint's command. The rat-faced clerk gave him a narrow-eyed look, and pointed to the back where the elderly clerk waited.

"You have a shipment for me?" Ben said as he approached the man.

"Yeah," the man said. "Four crates of rifles. They're in the back."

Ben followed the man to the rear of the building. Four large crates, marked 'Carbine, Springfield, 16 each' sat on the loading dock.

"Funny, them rifles comin' in from San Francisco," the man said. "I thought the Springfield Armory was back east."

"These were some extra weapons one of the army units in California had," Ben said, using the cover story Wainwright had given him. "We got some new recruits, and they sent them to us."

"You gonna need some help with 'em. I tried to move one, and could barely budge it. Awful heavy for rifles."

"I think they put in a lot of packing so they wouldn't be damaged in shipment," Ben said. "My men and I can handle it."

The two wagons came around the corner of the building. With some effort, Davis and Layton got the rear ends close to the edge of the loading dock, so that they were able, with help from Ben, Hightower, and Buckley, to slide two crates onto each wagon. They drove back around to the front while Ben went inside to sign for the crates.

As they drove away, Ben didn't see the rat-faced clerk looking suspiciously at the way the springs on the wagons had compressed under the weight of the crates.

Back at Fort Marcy, Ben set to work putting his plan in motion.

He had the four crates moved to the

wagon he'd rented from the saloon keeper, and then covered with a layer of straw with a canvas covering over that. The oldest two of the men he'd hired were assigned to drive the wagon. He assigned Hightower and Buckley the duty of escorting it. They removed their uniforms, replacing them with the plain clothing like that worn by local ranch hands. Only if someone looked closely and noticed that they carried regulation army carbines and pistols would they know they were other than laborers ferrying a wagonload of hay. The remaining four men were dressed in cavalry uniforms, complete with carbines and pistols, and told that they were now part of the detachment, and would follow Ben's orders instantly. It was such a break from the menial jobs they usually did, they happily threw themselves into the spirit of it. It was, to them, a great adventure.

The rest of the afternoon was spent with Ben explaining quietly how his plan would work. If anyone at Fort March noticed that the detachment of ten had now grown to sixteen, and two wagon teams had become three, or if anyone wondered, they kept it to themselves.

Around midnight, a wagon pulled by four horses, with two men in the seat, drove through the gate of Fort Marcy. It rode low on its springs. Two other men in civilian clothing rode alongside the wagon as it turned south and headed for the edge of Santa Fe.

The streets the group traversed were empty at this time of night, with most of the activity centered around the central plaza and the saloons.

At sunup, after eating a quick breakfast and breaking camp, Ben had the two wagons lined up and the gear packed, and rode noisily through the gates. He turned southeast, following the main thoroughfare that connected with the Santa Fe Trail to the southeast of the city. Even early in the morning, the streets were becoming crowded with carriages, riders, and the sidewalks were beginning to fill with pedestrians.

Few of Santa Fe's residents were unaware of the cavalry formation riding through the streets. Several remarked at how low the wagons rode on their springs, and how tense and alert the ten soldiers looked, their heads swiveling continuously eyeing the people they passed, their weapons at the ready. One man in particular, a rodent-faced man with thinning hair, watched closely, and thought the soldiers were awful tense to just be transporting new rifles.

19.

The first hour went slowly as the convoy made its way along the trail which swung gently west.

Ben had Toussaint ride a few hundred yards ahead of the convoy and Scott off the trail and a hundred yards behind to watch for pursuers. He was especially wary when they approached the site of the previous attack, but they passed the area without incident.

He drove them hard, wanting to put as much distance between them and the city as possible, and hoping his cautions and planning would have been unnecessary; knowing, though, they hadn't been.

His emotions were split, and his mind was in turmoil. On the one hand, he worried about when and where robbers would strike them – and, he knew they would strike; they were too rich a target to ignore. On the other, he was concerned that the wagon escorted by Hightower and Buckley might have been detected. His stomach bubbled and the breakfast he'd hastily eaten threatened to come back up.

Approaching mid-day, they'd traveled over twenty miles, and the trail turned southeast. There was a flat plain to their north and northeast, stretching to the mountains to the north, and smaller foothills to their south. The prickling sensation at the base of Ben's skull told him that this was the perfect place for an ambush, but he could see ahead, far beyond George Toussaint, and the way was clear. Behind him, the land dipped a bit, but he could see more than a hundred yards in that direction, and it too looked clear.

Yet, he couldn't shake the itchy feeling; that sense that danger was near that had saved his life on more than one occasion in the past. He went over and over his plan in his mind. It seemed sound. Had he, he wondered, forgotten anything? Would the outlaws be able to anticipate his moves and outflank him? The questions that went through any soldier's mind before combat, especially the man in charge; his mistakes didn't just endanger him, they could cause the death of others.

Listening to the gurgling in his stomach, he regretted that second cup of coffee he'd had before leaving Fort Marcy.

20.

The hardest part of war is waiting. Once the shooting starts, the only consideration is survival. The experienced soldier puts fear on hold and automatically does what he has been trained to do in order to live.

The sight of George Toussaint galloping toward him shook Ben out of his self-induced funk. His senses were immediately on high alert.

He knew even before Toussaint arrived at his location what was about to happen, and what he had to do.

"Defensive formation," he yelled as he reined his horse in.

Malachi Davis, driving the lead wagon, jerked on the left rein, causing his team to veer left until his wagon was perpendicular to its original line of travel, while Hezekiah Layton jerked his in the opposite direction. Both men leapt from their seats, set the brakes, and unhitched the teams and led them between the wagons which now sat astride the trail. The five mounted troopers rode their horses into the space between the wagons, five of them facing east and four facing west.

He turned to look back along the trail. As he expected, Scott was galloping toward them. He guided his horse into the space between the wagons and took up his position facing west.

He hadn't had the opportunity to practice the maneuver, but was pleased that it had been executed almost flawlessly from his verbal directions. Even the men he'd hired in Santa Fe were moving smoothly, as if they'd worked with the detachment a long time.

Toussaint was the first to reach them. He took position with the group facing east.

"I saw ten or fifteen men up ahead, and they're ridin' this way," he said. "They's armed to the teeth."

As he finished, Scott arrived and stopped his horse next to Ben.

"Bunch of armed riders comin' at us, and ridin' hard," he said between gasps. "Must be near twenty of 'em."

"Hold your positions," Ben said. "Fire on my command."

Ben's voice was even. The itchy feeling at the base of his skull was gone now, replaced by the cold certainty of the battle to come.

As the riders from the west appeared over the horizon, he pulled his carbine from its saddle mount, checking to ensure there was a cartridge in the chamber. He could hear the whispering sounds around him of the others doing the same.

Looking over his shoulder, he saw another group approaching from the east.

He counted twenty riders, as Scott had said, in the group approaching from the west, and fifteen in the group from the east. The outlaws were taking no chances. They'd probably heard of Ben's defeat of the previous robbery attempt, and had decided to attack with overwhelming odds. They would probably be armed with the Winchester repeating rifles, assuming this would give them further advantage against the cavalrymen with their single-shot Springfields. Thirty-five to twelve with superior firepower would normally ensure victory to the numerically superior force. What losses the outlaws suffered would only mean a bigger share of the loot for the survivors.

The outlaws, though, hadn't factored in Ben's surprise.

When he estimated the larger group, coming from the west, was about eight hundred yards off, he tapped Layton on the shoulder.

"Get ready," he said. The young trooper climbed up on the wagon, pulling aside the canvas cover and dropped inside the bed. Ben turned to Davis and nodded. "You too, Malachi."

Davis removed the canvas cover and eased over the side into the wagon he'd been driving. The two troopers each hefted a Gatling gun, adjusted the tripod, and aimed it over the side of the wagon.

"Hold fire until I give the signal," Ben said. "The rest of you, dismount and lay low."

Everyone else jumped from their horses, carbines in hand, and lay prone on the ground beneath the wagons.

When the two groups of outlaws were just under five hundred yards away, Ben saw puffs of smoke followed quickly by the sharp crack of rifles as they opened fire.

"Open fire," he yelled.

He carefully aimed his carbine at the center of the oncoming group of riders, but before he could squeeze the trigger, he was almost deafened by the 'br-r-rp!' of the Gatling gun's six rotating barrels, spitting out 200 .58 caliber rounds per minute from the loading tray, as Layton turned the crank. This was followed quickly by the sound of Davis's gun firing.

The rounds, powered by black powder, and primed with percussion caps, slammed into men and horses alike as Layton swung it from left to right, and then back. Ben saw six men tumble from the saddle, and another three fall as their horses were struck. He took aim at the remaining riders and squeezed off a round. He was rewarded with the man pitching over the back of his saddle.

Now the other troopers were firing their carbines; the cavalry troopers firing methodically, extracting the spent cartridge and quickly reloading to fire again, the four hired men firing a bit more raggedly. Layton continued to rake the oncoming formation with deadly effect.

Forward momentum kept the outlaws moving forward for over a hundred yards, during which nearly half their number were struck, either by the Gatling gun or by carbine fire. They were under four hundred yards away when the gravity of the situation dawned on them and their forward progress stopped. Their formation began to break up, and several wheeled their horses around and began riding back toward the west. Others fled north and south in an effort to escape the deadly accurate fire of the troopers' carbines.

Ben took advantage of the lack of fire from the approaching outlaws to turn and look toward the east. The band coming from that direction had suffered even more. Davis had proven to be as deadly accurate with the rapid firing Gatling as he was with a carbine, and along with the fire from the carbines, had reduced that group to five riders who had turned and were now fleeing for their lives.

When Ben turned his attention back to the west, he noted that the survivors of that group had also decided to flee. He counted ten still in the saddle. Suddenly, the fleeing outlaws pulled their horses up, and put their hands in the air.

Over the rise, just beyond them, another band of ten horsemen rode. Ben looked puzzled, until he recognized the tall man dressed in black riding in the center of that group.

"Cease fire," he ordered.

The shooting stopped. The only sound was

the ragged breathing of the men lying on the ground under the wagons. The acrid smell of gun powder hung in the air.

The new arrivals rode up to the surrendering outlaws and disarmed them. The entire group then galloped up to the wagons. Ben stood to greet them.

"Mr. Palladin," he said. "I didn't expect to see you way out here."

Palladin touched a finger to the brim of his black hat.

"I was buyin' some provisions at the general store when you fellas rode out," he said. "When I saw a big group of gunmen ridin' out about thirty minutes after you, I kind of figured you might need a little help." He inclined his head toward a beefy man with stringy brown hair and a droopy mustache who rode next to him. "I convinced Marshal Deeds here to put together a posse and we come out to lend a hand. You didn't leave us much, though."

"That one of them there Gatlin' guns?" the marshal asked. "Damnation, it do pack a wallop. Some of them boys tore all to pieces."

"After our experience last time," Ben said. "I thought I'd come prepared."

"You must be carryin' somethin' awful valuable to cause a gang this size to come after you."

"Just supplies and weapons," Ben said, sticking to the story Wainwright had given him.

Palladin nodded, but regarded Ben closely.

"Sure. Guess these boys got some bad information. You know that rat-faced clerk at the depot is the one who put 'em on to you."

"We captured one of the outlaws who tried to rob us last time, and he said it was someone at the depot, but he didn't know who."

"Yup," the marshal said. "Henry Carson. He's cousin to a good-for-nothin' named Deke Slater. Slater runs most of the gang activity 'round Santa Fe. Him and Henry got a good deal goin'; least ways, they *had* a good deal 'till now. Henry'd tell Deke when valuable shipments were comin' in, and who they were goin' to, and Deke'd put together a gang and steal it. It was workin' pretty good 'till you busted up their attempt to steal the army payroll. Guess they thought they'd make it up on this."

"Well, they were wasting their time coming after us," Ben said. "Nothing here worth stealing."

Palladin continued to regard Ben

skeptically for a moment, and then he laughed.

"Right, sergeant, nothin' at all. Just shows how stupid crooks can be. Well, I reckon you'll be wantin' to get your *supplies* to the fort."

Palladin winked at Ben as if to say, I know what you're doing. And, it's pretty smart.

"We got time to help you bury the dead," Ben said.

"That's powerful nice of you," Marshal Deed said. "But, I reckon this bunch we captured can do that." He turned, and pointed to five men to his left. "Ya'll take this bunch and round up the carcasses and have 'em start diggin' graves. The rest of us'll light out after the others who got away. You git done 'fore we git back, jest take 'em back to Santa Fe and lock 'em up."

Ben's gaze locked with Palladin's.

"Mr. Palladin," he said. "Looks like I owe you once again."

Palladin once again touched a finger to his hat brim.

"My pleasure. 'Sides, I reckon there'll be at least two or three of these boys got a bounty on his head; and even havin' to split it with the posse, it ain't a bad day's work."

He then pressed his knee against his horse's shoulder, pulling it around and trailed off after the marshal without looking back.

"That is one strange and scary man," Toussaint said.

"Yeah," Ben said. "I'm just glad he's on our side."

21.

They rode on until near sundown, and made camp about thirty miles west of Las Vegas. Ben posted four guards in four-hour shifts.

The next morning, he roused everyone just before sunrise.

"I figure we can make Las Vegas by sundown if we get an early start," he said as they sat around the cook fire waiting for the breakfast of ham, beans, and biscuits that Tom Holman was cooking.

"You think the other wagon'll be there by now?" Toussaint asked.

Ben shook his head.

"It was pretty loaded, and they have to cover more miles," he said. "They'll probably be a day behind us."

"Provided they didn't run into no trouble."

Toussaint's dark face look troubled.

"Samuel and Charles know how to take care of themselves." Ben wished that he felt as confident as he sounded. Truth was, as soon as the gunfight with the outlaws was over, he'd started worrying about the other wagon.

"You know," Toussaint said. "We ain't likely to run into more trouble 'tween here and the fort. Word gone git out that we got Gatlin' guns. Ain't no more outlaws likely to want to tangle with us."

"What are you suggesting?"

"Well, I'se thinkin' maybe I take Journeyman and Lucas, and we cut 'cross country and hook up with the other wagon. Three more rifles wouldn't hurt just in case somebody decides to make a try for 'em."

Ben took a sip of coffee, pondering Toussaint's suggestion. It was true. They were unlikely to be bothered again. Not even the most desperate outlaw would want to face two Gatling guns. Knowing the bullion was guarded by five carbines rather than just two would also put his mind at ease.

"Okay," he said. "Soon's you finish eating, you three take off. We'll wait for you in Las Vegas. We'll be at the hotel near the livery stable on the south side of town."

Toussaint, Keller and Hall left, riding south, before the rest of the group had finished eating. As soon as the last bite of food was gone, and the hired men made sure of that, Ben had the camp struck, and they resumed their journey to Las Vegas.

The convoy arrived in Las Vegas two hours before sundown. Ben posted two soldiers to guard the wagons at the livery stable, and then talked the hotel next door into renting him seven rooms. After establishing the guard rotation schedule, he left the men to their own devices, warning them to stay out of the town's saloons.

The four civilians had never been more than ten miles away from Santa Fe in their lives, and even though Ben's injunction hadn't applied to them, they decided to stay near the troopers. Ben could understand their reluctance to wander the streets of Las Vegas. When darkness fell, the lights of dozens of saloons blazed and the streets were awash with cowboys in various stages of inebriation, all armed, and many spoiling for a fight.

After supper, Ben sat in a rocking chair on the rickety wooden sidewalk in front of the hotel in the shadow of the sign that hung askance from the canopy overhanging the sidewalk. He watched cowboys staggering or swaggering by, some alone, some in the company of the ladies of the evening who, while they too staggered, Ben knew they were cold sober and waiting for an opportunity to separate their drunken companions from whatever money they had in their pockets. Many a cowboy would wake up in the morning in an alley with a powerful headache and an empty pocket. Ben wasn't anxious to get back to the boredom of Fort Union, but even that was preferable to the wild streets of most of the territory's towns.

He found that he couldn't sit still, so he got up and walked to the livery stable to check on the guards. Then, back to the rocking chair. He did this until just about midnight, when he realized that exhausting himself wouldn't ensure the safety of his five troops, that he needed to trust that they knew what they were doing, and besides, there was nothing he could do to influence events. He finally gave up and went to his room. He lay on top of the bed clothes, having removed only his boots, and he tossed and turned for an hour before finally falling asleep.

His sleep was fitful, though, and he woke with the sun the next morning, as tired as if he'd stayed awake all night. His eyes felt gritty and his mouth was dry. Even brushing his teeth and splashing cold water on his face didn't help. He kept his expression neutral around the others, but his stomach roiled, and the eggs and ham served in the hotel's dining room were tasteless. He mostly picked at his food and drank coffee.

After breakfast, he went back to the rocking chair in front of the hotel. He sat and he rocked, and he kept his eyes on the road coming from the south. He hardly noticed the people who passed him on the sidewalk, many of whom viewed him with suspicion, wondering why a soldier had taken up residence in front of a building in their town. No one spoke to him, though. The expression on his brown face made it clear that he wanted no conversation.

Just when Ben thought he could bear it no longer, and was about to get his horse and go in search of the missing wagon, a creaking wagon and five riders came around a bend in the street to the south. Ben's heart leapt as he recognized the broad-shouldered figure of George Toussaint in the vanguard of the riders.

He sprang from the chair and ran to the livery stable, arriving just as they did.

"I was beginning to think you fellas had gotten lost," he said, trying to inject a hint of humor into his voice.

"Naw, we didn't get lost," Hightower said. "Matter of fact, we was pushin' pretty hard; didn't even stop and make camp. We just pulled off the trail and rested a spell ever now and then. We'd of made it here last night, but one of the wheels come off and we lost four hours fixin' it."

"That's what they was doin' when we caught up to 'em," Toussaint said.

"So, other than a thrown wheel, did you have any trouble?"

"Naw, went smooth as fresh cream. George told us ya'll had a bit of a dust up, though. Guess bringin' them Gatlin' guns along was a good idea after all."

Ben nodded.

"Reckon that's a fact. Say, you fellas tired, or you think you're up to making a run for the fort today?"

"If we start now," Hightower said. "We just might make it in time for supper."

22.

They pushed hard, but were twenty minutes after supper arriving at Fort Union. Ben had the men see to their mounts while he delivered the wagon of bullion to Major Wainwright. News of their arrival, and their exploits, quickly spread throughout the fort. The mess sergeant, though, reopened the mess and served them steaks, beans, biscuits and gravy, and hot coffee when he heard what they'd gone through. He even included the six hired civilians in the feast.

They pushed two tables together to make room for all sixteen to sit together. As they ate, troopers from all over the fort dropped by the table to congratulate them on beating off a force twice their size. Several men wanted to shake Ben's hand, including a few of the other line sergeants.

During one of the rare moments when they weren't being besieged by admirers, one of the younger men Ben had hired turned to Ben.

"Sergeant, how come you to join the army?" he asked.

Ben told him about growing up in East Texas, and learning that the army had organized a unit in New Orleans for black soldiers. All six of the civilians were mouth agape when Ben told them he'd walked from upper East Texas to New Orleans to enlist.

"You wanted to be a soldier that bad?" one of the older men asked.

"I'm not sure it's because I wanted to be a soldier," Ben said. "I just didn't want to be a farmer."

"I hear that," the man said. "But, there ain't that many jobs for a colored man out here 'cept farmin' or workin' on a ranch doin' all the jobs the white folk don't want to do."

"You know," the young man said. "This is the first time I done been mo than thirty mile from where I was born. Ya'll done seen so much. It must be somethin'."

"It's hard sometimes," Toussaint, who was sitting next to the young man, said. "We out here to protect folk, but most of 'em don't even think of us as men."

"How you deal with that?"

"You just ignore it," Ben said. "And, do your job."

One of the other men nodded.

"It ain't no different for us," he said. "White folk out here rate us jest above Injuns, and below horses. 'Least you cavalry fellas git to carry guns, and when somebody mess wit you, you can shoot back."

"Yeah," the youngster said. "Like you done them outlaws. Man, that was sho somethin'."

"But, it's nothing to be happy about," Ben said. "We don't kill because we want to, or like it. We do it to protect ourselves or others."

The young man's face contorted as he concentrated on Ben's words. Then, he smiled.

"You do it 'cause it yo duty, right?"

"That's right. Because it's your duty."

"Look here, sergeant," he said. "I been doin' me some thinkin', and I'se wondering . . . uh, how can I join up and become a soldier like you?"

Toussaint clapped the young man on the shoulder, laughing.

"Boy, you be a long time 'fore you can be half the soldier Ben Carter is. You got a long way to go 'fore you can even be half as good as me, and as much as I hate to admit it, I'm 'bout half what Ben is."

Ben and Toussaint had become friends over time, but this was the first time the big sergeant had ever praised him like that. Ben felt his cheeks flush.

"Hell fire, George, you're just as good as me, and you know it."

"Well, 'course I knows that," he said, and winked. "Just wanted to impress the civilian, and let him know it ain't easy learnin' to be a soldier."

Everyone around the table laughed, Ben included.

"If you're really serious, son," he said. "I'll talk to the major in the morning and see if he's recruiting new men."

The young man beamed and puffed out his chest.

"I'se dead serious. I want to be a soldier."

23.

Ben found empty bunks in a barracks near his and arranged for the six civilians to sleep there, after promising again to talk to the commander about enlisting the young man. The others, along with the wagon and team, would be escorted back to Santa Fe.

When he returned to his barracks, his men were waiting for him, grouped around his bunk. The smiles and happiness of the mess were gone.

"What's wrong?" he asked.

And, they told him. They were, to a man, tired of garrison duty. They wanted to be back in the field where they belonged; where any proper cavalry trooper belonged. They asked, no demanded, that Ben ask the commander to give them a patrol assignment. Chasing renegade Indians or outlaws was preferable to being set to tending laborers or driving cattle.

"If I wanted to do that," Buckley said. "I'd of stayed on the ranch instead of joinin' the army."

"You got to do somethin', Ben," Toussaint said. "We stay here too long, and we lose our edge. We fightin' soldiers, not garrison soldiers."

Ben wasn't sure how Major Wainwright would react, but as the leader of his unit, he had a responsibility to his men. And, he too was tired of being cooped up in the fort, tired of the details that amounted to little more than tending chickens.

"Okay," he said. "I'll talk to the commander first thing in the morning."

There were nods and smiles. They trusted him to do the right thing. He didn't want to think about how they'd react if he failed.

When he finally undressed and fell into bed, he soon forgot to worry about it. For the first time in weeks, he slept peacefully.

The next morning, after breakfast call at 6:30, as he walked toward Wainwright's office, he remembered, and the worry came back.

The vulpine smile on the major's face didn't reassure him.

"Sit down, sergeant," Wainwright said.

"You look like you got something on your mind."

Ben agreed that he did. He first mentioned the young civilian who wanted to enlist. Wainwright said that he didn't need any new troopers, but the commander at Fort Stanton was recruiting. He promised to check into it. Then, Ben asked if his detachment could be assigned field duty, and waited for the major to say 'no.'

"Well, Sergeant Carter," Wainwright said, still smiling. "It's funny you should bring that up. I do have a field assignment coming up, and I think you and your men would be perfect for it."

"Sir, we aren't really cut out for garrison – uh, you have a field assignment for us?" Ben couldn't believe his ears.

"I do, and I think you just might like it too."

"As long as it gets me and my men in the field, I reckon it'll be fine, sir."

"There's just one thing about the mission, though . . . you'll have to take some civilians along with you."

"Civilians? What kind of mission would we be doing that involves civilians, sir? Surveying a road or something?"

Ben knew that on occasion the cavalry had to escort parties of surveyors and engineers who were building the roads and railroads that were linking the eastern half of the country to the growing west. He'd just about had his fill of escort duty, but if it was away from the fort, it would be bearable.

"Well," Wainwright said. "They are surveyors of a type, but not roads."

He explained that there were people in the west and back east who wanted to set aside part of the territory as parks where people could go and enjoy the natural scenery and wildlife. They'd already established one national park up in Montana Territory in 1872, at a place called Yellowstone. Now, he said, they were looking at a place in central California; Yosemite. A group of engineers were coming to survey and catalog the area before asking the Congress to declare it a park.

"The problem is, though," he continued. "A lot of people out here, mostly ranchers, miners and timber interests, oppose it. They see the land as something to use to get rich off of, and they're willing to use violence, so the surveying parties need protection."

"Seems strange," Ben said. "We're usually protecting the ranchers and miners. Sounds to me like this time we might have to be fighting them."

Wainwright nodded. His craggy face looked sad. But, it could come to that, he knew. Money made people do strange things. He wasn't sure where his sympathies lay in the dispute over the parks. On the one hand, he felt that people who could tame the land should have the right to do so. On the other, he'd seen what mining and logging could do when money was the only objective; vast tracts of land laid bare and worthless for generations because of uncontrolled mining or timber cutting.

"Let's hope you don't have to," Wainwright said. "This area in California is pretty far from where most of the companies are working at the moment. Maybe you won't run into trouble there. But, if you do, just remember your mission; protect the survey team. They're being sent out here by the president."

"You can count on us, sir. That team will be as safe as a babe in its mother's arms."

"I have to warn you about the team, sergeant; they're a bunch of engineers mostly. I reckon they're accustomed to being in the wild, but they might not be quite as disciplined as your soldiers. You'll need to handle them carefully."

Ben didn't figure they could be any more

difficult than a bunch of raw recruits, or hired civilians; or, even worse, a herd of cattle. He'd handled all that and survived. He would figure out how to deal with these engineers.

"Understood, sir," he said.

"Good. Now, the team will be arriving in November, two months from now. That means you'll be traveling during winter over some pretty rough terrain. So, you'll need to spend the time between now and then mapping out a route to get you there and back."

Ben did the figures in his head. Doing reconnaissance of a route from Fort Union to California, which would mean riding it at least part way, and back would take over a month, and then escorting the team would take longer. He and his team could be in the field for four or five months.

"I'll get the men ready right away, sir," Ben said, smiling.

Ben saluted crisply and headed back for his barracks. There was a spring in his step, and a feeling of ease in his mind that hadn't been there since the second day of their 'easy' garrison duty.

As he walked, his mind was occupied with all the things he'd have to do. They would need to draw extra gear, ammunition, rations, and horses for the reconnaissance. Part of the way, he knew, was across desert and part over mountain, so they would need gear for both hot and cold weather. They would need remounts, maybe one extra horse per man, and pack animals, preferably mules, because they're more sure-footed than horses over rough terrain, but can carry just as much weight.

When he entered the barracks, nine faces turned and regarded him with expectant looks.

He stood in the center of the room for a long time, his hands on his hips, letting the suspense build. He maintained a stoic expression.

When they could take it no longer, George Toussaint planted himself in front of Ben, a scowl creasing his broad brow.

"That look of yours say you got bad news, Ben," he said. "What is it this time? We gone have to herd sheep?"

At the plaintive look on the man's face, Ben could hold back no longer. The laughter exploded from him. He doubled over, hugging his sides.

"What in Sam hell so funny?" Toussaint asked.

Finally, Ben was able to get control of himself. He smiled at his second in command.

"The look on your face, that's what," he said. "If you could see it, you'd laugh too. All of you, for that matter, look like prisoners waiting for the hangman. Well, you can wipe those frowns off your face. We're going back into the field."

Toussaint's scowl was replaced by a look of puzzlement and then a broad smile.

"Sho nuff? Now, that was mean of you to make us worry like that, Ben Carter. But, I forgive you. Where we goin'; what we gone be doin'?"

Ben told them.

The cheers from the barracks could be heard from one side of the fort to another.

24.

They were a week into the reconnaissance mission, and had crossed most of New Mexico and Arizona Territories. They were riding up a slope toward a range of mountains to the northwest that seemed to offer the most direct route to their destination in California.

Ben had chosen a route that curled south of the mountains north of Santa Fe, and then north toward the Arizona-Utah border, bypassing populated areas as much as possible, while still looking for trails that could be easily traveled by wagons, for he assumed that the surveyors would have several wagons carrying their equipment.

Even though the detachment's size had swelled, with the extra horses and pack mules, they managed 45 miles a day easily. Ben made note, though, of possible camp sites every twenty miles or so, figuring they'd not be able to move as fast with the civilians.

It was their first time in northern Arizona, and every man in the detachment was awed by the scenery – vast plains covered with the towering saguaro cactus plants, some up to thirty feet high and six feet in circumference at the base, snow-covered mountains looming over the desert below, and brilliant colors, red, brown, pink, and green, everywhere. Now and then, they would come over a rise and find themselves looking down at an emerald green lake ringed by jagged, cactus-covered hills, or encounter a river meandering southward toward Mexico, carving small valleys in the arid, rocky soil.

Everyone was excited about the prospect of seeing California, but none more so than Ben. He would at last, he hoped, get a chance to see an ocean. He'd gotten a glimpse of the Gulf of Mexico when he enlisted in the cavalry in New Orleans, but he'd heard stories about the vast oceans to the east and west, and had dreamed of seeing them since he was a child living in the pine-covered red clay hills of East Texas.

Ben and George Toussaint were standing on the eastern rim of the beginning of what appeared to be a long canyon that ran toward the northwest. Their horses grazed on sweet grass just below where they stood. The rest of the detachment waited on the trail fifty yards below them.

"You reckon we should go 'round the east or west side of this canyon?" Toussaint asked.

Ben looked north. From where they stood the canyon didn't look like much, but the peaks to the north looked jagged and suggested an extensive range of mountains. The river running through the center of the canyon, some fifty feet below them, raced swiftly, indicating some pressure upstream, possibly heavy rapids. If the canyon was long, going east would add to their journey. To the west, though, Ben had heard there was a great desert, which would also cause them to have to waste time bypassing it.

But, the western route was the most direct one to their destination, and the one likely to be easier for a wagon train.

"I reckon we should go west," he said.

"What about that desert? They call it Death Valley, 'cause so many people tryin' to cross it is just bleached bones now."

"Well, we can always keep going west until we're past the desert, and then turn north."

Toussaint beamed.

"Yeah, maybe we gets to see that Pacific

Ocean."

"Maybe we will," Ben agreed.

"I can't wait to see San Francisco," Toussaint said. "They say it prettier than any city on earth."

"I haven't seen many cities, so I can't say. I hear it is pretty, though."

"This here's pretty country, too. I can see why them fellas back east want to save it. Folks ought to see the country like God made it."

"True," Ben said. "We need farms and mines and such, but it would be nice to have places where a man can go and just look at the trees and animals once and a while."

"And, just think, Ben; we be a part of that. Now, ain't that somethin'?"

It is indeed, thought Ben, it is indeed.

Then, he heard something he'd never thought to hear. Standing next to him, Toussaint was humming a tune in his deep baritone voice,

Look way over yonder, what do I see –

Meet me at de sunrise in de mornin'.

Dere's a little band of angels, lookin' at me.

Meet me at de sunrise in de mornin'.

Ben sighed. All was right with the world again.

Charles Ray

Author's Note

Popular media has portrayed the U.S. Cavalry as mostly on long patrols looking for hostile Indians, or battling those Indians. While the movies and TV shows haven't shown the men of the Ninth and Tenth Cavalry (or the 24th and 25th Infantry Regiments) in their true role, the fact is, what they do show is inaccurate.

Most of a cavalry trooper's life was spent in garrison at one of the many forts that dotted the western frontier after the Civil War. While they did spend a lot of time chasing and fighting Indians and outlaws, the less than glamorous camp life was what they spent most of their time doing. This involved foraging for timber and food, fighting fires in the forts, taking care of animals and equipment, and training. Off duty life often consisted of frequenting the tent cities of liquor purveyors, gamblers, and prostitutes that sprang up around the forts. In many ways, life for the frontier soldier was not dissimilar to that I recall during my own army service from 1962 to 1982, serving at posts in Oklahoma, California, Arizona, Georgia, and North Carolina – we spent a lot of time 'hurrying up and waiting.'

A trooper's day often began with first call, or reveille, just before 6:00 a.m., and ended with taps at around 8:00 p.m. The day would be filled with fatigue, or work details, drill, and parades. Fatigue duty could be anything from picking vegetables from the fort garden to repair or construction of the fort's buildings. Woodcutting details to get timber for various purposes were quite common.

For a good account of garrison life for a cavalry trooper, I recommend *New Mexico's Buffalo Soldiers: 1866 – 1900,* by Monroe Lee Billington, and published in 1991 by the University Press of Colorado. This book is available on Amazon.com at:

http://www.amazon.com/New-Mexicos-Buffalo-Soldiers-1866-1900/dp/0870813463/

in paperback, and is an excellent beginning volume for anyone interested in the history of the Buffalo Soldiers.

The Buffalo Soldier series:

Buffalo Soldier: Trial by Fire
Buffalo Soldier: Homecoming
Buffalo Soldier: Incident at Cactus Junction
Buffalo Soldier: Peacekeepers
Buffalo Soldier: Renegade
Buffalo Soldier: Escort Duty

Other books by this author:

Al Pennyback mysteries

Color Me Dead
Memorial to the Dead
Deadline
Dead, White, and Blue
A Good Day to Die
The Day the Music Died
Die, Sinner
Deadly Intentions
Death by Design
Till Death Do Us Part
Deadly Dose
Dead Man's Cove
Dead Men Don't Answer
Deadly Paradise
Kiss of Death
The Last Gunfighters

Other fiction

Angel on His Shoulder
She's No Angel
Child of the Flame
Pip's Revenge
Wallace in Underland
Further Adventures of Wallace in Underland
Dead Letter and Other Tales
The White Dragons
The Dragon's Lair

Nonfiction

Things I Learned from My Grandmother About Leadership and Life
Taking Charge: Effective Leadership for the Twenty-first Century
Grab the Brass ring
African Places: A Photographic Journey Through Zimbabwe and southern Africa

About the Author

Charles Ray has been writing fiction since his teens. He won a Sunday school magazine writing contest when he was thirteen, and having his byline on a short story published in a national publication forever hooked him on writing. During his time in the army (1962-1982) he often moonlighted as a newspaper or magazine journalist, and was the editorial cartoonist for the Spring Lake (NC) News, a weekly newspaper, during the 1970s. In addition to his writing, he was an artist/cartoonist and photographer for a number of publications, including Ebony, Eagle and Swan, and Essence, and had a monthly cartoon feature and did several covers for Buffalo, a now-defunct magazine that was dedicated to showcasing the contributions of African-Americans to the country's military history.

After retiring from the army, he joined the U.S. Foreign Service, and served as a diplomat in posts in Asia and Africa until his retirement in 2012. He has worked and traveled throughout the world (Antarctica is the only continent he hasn't visited), and now, as a full time writer, continues to globetrot looking for interesting things to write about, draw, or take pictures of.

A native of Texas, he now calls Maryland

home. For more on his writing and other projects, check one of the following Web sites:

http://redroom.com/member/charles-a-ray
http://charlesaray.blogspot.com
http://charlieray45.wordpress.com
http://www.twitter.com/charlieray45
http://www.facebook.com/charlieray45
http://www.flickr.com/photos/charlesray45/
http://www.viewbug.com/member/charlesray